# EXTRA CREDIT

## Also by Andrew Clements

# EXTRA CREDIT

## Andrew Clements
### Illustrations by Mark Elliott

**Atheneum Books for Young Readers**

New York · London · Toronto · Sydney

ATHENEUM BOOKS FOR YOUNG READERS

An imprint of Simon & Schuster Children's Publishing Division

1230 Avenue of the Americas, New York, New York 10020

Text copyright © 2009 by Andrew Clements

Illustrations copyright © 2009 by Mark Elliott

All rights reserved, including the right of reproduction in whole or in part in any form.

ATHENEUM BOOKS FOR YOUNG READERS is a registered trademark of Simon & Schuster, Inc.

For information about special discounts for bulk purchases, please contact Simon & Schuster Special Sales at 1-866-506-1949 or business@simonandschuster.com.

The Simon & Schuster Speakers Bureau can bring authors to your live event. For more information or to book an event, contact the Simon & Schuster Speakers Bureau at 1-866-248-3049 or visit our website at www.simonspeakers.com.

Also available in an Atheneum Books for Young Readers hardcover edition

Book design by Russell Gordon

The text for this book is set in Bembo.

The illustrations for this book are rendered in pencil.

Manufactured in the United States of America

0815 OFF

First Atheneum Books for Young Readers paperback edition February 2011

10  9

The Library of Congress has cataloged the hardcover edition as follows:

Clements, Andrew, 1949–

Extra credit / Andrew Clements; illustrations by Mark Elliott. —1st ed.

p. cm.

Summary: As letters flow back and forth—between the prairies of Illinois and the mountains of Afghanistan, across cultural and religious divides—sixth-grader Abby, ten-year-old Amira, and eleven-year-old Sadeed begin to speak and listen to one another.

ISBN 978-1-4169-4929-9 (hc)

[1. Letters—Fiction. 2. Pen pals—Fiction. 3. Family life—Afghanistan—Fiction. 4. Family life—Illinois—Fiction. 5. Afghanistan—Fiction. 6. Illinois—Fiction.] I. Elliott, Mark, 1967– ill. II. Title.

PZ7.C59118Ex 2009

[Fic]—dc22

2008042877

ISBN 978-1-4169-4931-2 (pbk)

*For Rick Richter*

# CHAPTER 1

# IN THE HILLS ABOVE KABUL

Sadeed knew he wasn't supposed to be listening to the men talking in the next room. He also knew he wasn't supposed to be peeking through the crack near the bottom of the old wooden door. But they had to be talking about him in there—why else would his teacher have invited him to the home of the headman of the village?

His teacher, Mahmood Jafari, had not told him much. "Please come to Akbar Khan's house this afternoon at four. He and his councillors meet today, and I have to speak with them. And I may need you to be there."

Sadeed thought perhaps his teacher was going to recommend him for a special honor. That wasn't hard to imagine, not at all. Perhaps the village elders would award him a scholarship to one of the finest new schools in Kabul. He would wear blue trousers and a clean white shirt to classes every day, and he would have his own computer, and he would take his place as one of the future leaders of Afghanistan. His father and mother would be very proud of him. It would be a great opportunity. And Sadeed was certain he richly deserved it.

Through the crack in the door, Sadeed could see all seven men, sitting on cushions around a low table, sipping tea. An electric bulb hung overhead, and two wires ran across the ceiling to the gasoline generator outside. Mahmood was talking to Akbar Khan, but the teacher's back was toward the door, and Sadeed couldn't hear what he was saying.

When the teacher finished, someone Sadeed knew—Hassan Jaji—began to speak. Hassan stopped by his father's shop in the village bazaar at least once a week, and he sometimes stayed awhile, telling stories about his time as a freedom fighter during the war with the Soviet Union. One day he had shown Sadeed where a Russian grenade had blown two fingers off his right hand.

And as the man spoke now, that was the hand he used to stroke his chin.

"I am only a simple man," Hassan said, "and I would never try to stop progress. But our traditions protect us. And they protect our children. And I believe that the schoolteacher has asked us to allow something that would not be proper."

The eyes of the men turned back to Mahmood. The teacher looked around the circle and cleared his throat, speaking more forcefully now so that Sadeed could hear every word he said. "What Hassan says about our traditions is certainly true."

He paused, and Sadeed saw him hold up a bright green envelope with three stamps on it, each one a small picture of an American flag. The front of the envelope was decorated with two pink butterfly stickers.

The teacher said, "But it is also a tradition that we are a courteous people. And therefore one student from our village school must answer this letter from the girl in America. And I believe it would be *most* courteous if our very best student writes back, the one student who is most skillful with the English language. And that one student is Sadeed Bayat."

A pang of disappointment cut through Sadeed.

His name had just been spoken in the ears of the most important men in this part of Panjshir Province, and why? To be recommended for a great honor? No. To write a letter. To a girl.

Hassan stroked his chin again. He shook his head. "That letter is from an American girl. And should a boy and a girl be sharing their thoughts this way? No. Let one of the girls write back. A girl would be more proper."

And outside the door, Sadeed nodded and whispered, "Exactly!"

The teacher spoke up again. "To be sure, what Hassan says would be best. But the letter that goes back to America will represent our village, even our nation. And should we accept less than the very best writing, the best spelling and grammar? I know Sadeed Bayat—you may know him too, the son of Zakir the wheat merchant. He is a good boy. And his excellent writing will represent us well. His words will speak well of all the children of Afghanistan. And I feel sure that no harm will come of this. I feel sure that—"

Akbar Khan held up a hand, and Mahmood went silent.

The headman said, "Have you told Sadeed about this letter yet?"

"No," said the teacher. "I came to ask for advice."

Akbar nodded. "You did well to wait." The headman looked around the circle. "I agree that the finest student from our village must reply. And I agree that it would be best if a girl from our school is the writer." Akbar turned to the teacher. "Sadeed has a sister, doesn't he?"

"Yes," Mahmood said. "Amira, about two years younger."

The headman smiled. "Just so. Amira will write back to the girl in America. And the finest student from our village will watch over her and help her, doing what is needed to be sure that the writing is excellent. But only the girl will sign the letter. And therefore, all will be proper. And, of course, our teacher promises that nothing shameful will come of this." Looking Mahmood full in the face, he said, "Do you promise this?"

Mahmood nodded. "I do."

"Then it is decided," said Akbar Khan. "And now we will have more tea."

Fifteen minutes later, when his teacher came out into the entry hall, Sadeed was sitting on the long wooden bench with two men who had arrived to speak before the village elders. He stood up and followed his teacher down the hallway, out the door, across the walled courtyard, and then through the iron gate that opened onto the main road.

As they stood beside the road, Mahmood smiled and said, "Thank you for coming, Sadeed. It turns out that I needn't have bothered you. I know you need to hurry to your job now, but I must speak with you before school tomorrow morning. I need your help with an important job."

Sadeed nodded, taking care to put a puzzled look on his face.

"So," Mahmood said. "Good evening."

And with a small, formal bow, the teacher turned right and walked toward the school, headed home. Not only did he work at the school, but he lived in a room built against the rear wall of the building.

Sadeed turned in the other direction, headed back toward the bazaar. He worked for his father every day after school, and the shop would be open for at least another hour.

As he walked along the road, following a large man riding on a small donkey, he thought about all he had heard. No great honors were heading his way. However, Akbar Khan himself had

7

called him "the finest student from our village."
So that was good.

And Sadeed also thought about tomorrow, about how he would have to pretend to be surprised when his teacher told him he must help Amira—just like he had pretended to be puzzled a few moments ago.

But the only thing that actually puzzled Sadeed was how his teacher could call writing a letter to a girl in America "an important job."

Because *that* made no sense at all.

# CHAPTER 2

# IN THE HILLS
# ABOVE LINSDALE

It was a long way down, but Abby tried not to think about it. She dug the rubber toes of her rock-climbing shoes deeper into the crevice. She tested the grip of her left hand, then arched her back and stretched her right arm above the ledge, feeling around for something she could grab onto.

Reaching made the strap of her helmet pull tighter against her chin. A bead of sweat trickled down her forehead, gained speed, then dripped off the tip of her nose and disappeared, far, far below. One slip, one false move, and this climb would be over. The rope might save her life, but a fall would mean defeat. It would mean this mountain had beaten her. And Abby would not accept that.

There wasn't a breath of wind, no cries from soaring eagles, no harsh sunshine, nothing to break her total concentration. And there was nothing in her way to the summit—except this two-foot ledge, this little gray overhang, scraping against the top of her helmet.

Her right hand found a bump overhead, a lump, and yes, there was an upside grip on it, wide enough for four fingers.

But if she let go with her left hand, and gave up both toeholds to increase her reach, could those four fingers of her right hand hold tight? And with her feet hanging, could she hold on long enough for her left hand to reach up and find another grip? And if her left hand *did* find a grip, would she have the strength to pull herself higher so she could get a new foothold?

There was only one way to find out.

Still holding on with her left hand, Abby reached down and pushed her right hand into the chalk bag hanging from the belt at her waist. The white powder scoured the sweat from her fingers, leaving them so dry they almost squeaked. She reached up again, took a firm grip with her right hand, let go with her left, and then stepped away from her toeholds, trying to keep her legs from swinging.

Hanging by just four fingers now, she tilted her head back, eyes searching above for a bump or a crack. And there it was. She pulled with her right arm, reached up with her left, but the second grip was still an inch too high—an inch that might as well have been a mile.

Her right-hand grip was failing, and Abby made a desperate grab with her left. But the effort made her legs swing, and that caused more strain on her aching fingers. And that was it.

She fell back and plunged straight down, a tenth of a second, then another. The rope stretched, then snapped taut and caught her. She spun wildly toward the gray wall, but she was ready, both hands on the rope now, her legs bent to absorb the shock.

Twenty-six feet below, Mr. Insley gave a blast on his whistle. "Jan, Carrie, let 'er down easy."

And five seconds later, Abby Carson had both feet on the floor next to the climbing wall in her first-period gym class.

It was probably the flatness of the land in central Illinois that had gotten Abby so excited about climbing. And she wasn't alone. Lots of other kids in town also had the climbing bug.

Her big brother, Tom, claimed that he and some friends had reached the peak of the town's water tower, more than 120 feet. It took Abby's breath away to think about being up that high— even if her brother's story about the daring climb, followed by a police chase through the cornfields, wasn't 100 percent true. He was known to tell some pretty tall tales.

But the massive concrete grain elevator by the railroad tracks at the edge of town? Someone had *definitely* climbed that thing. Because the person who got to the summit had left a mark: the name of the high school teams, painted near the top of the tallest silo. The word LIONS was so big that other teams coming to town could see it while their buses were still five miles away.

However, in the town of Linsdale, the thirty-foot wall in the gym at Baldridge Elementary School was the tallest man-made thing a kid could climb on—without getting into trouble with the law.

The wall had been installed a week before Thanksgiving, and instantly it had become Abby's favorite thing about school. Ever. And before Christmas vacation, she had mastered every route to the top—except the path that led to the overhanging ledge. Here she was in the first week of March, and it still blocked her way. Six times she had tried to beat the ledge, and six times she had failed.

Even so, Abby loved that wall. She loved the brightly colored grips spaced out across the dark gray surface. She loved making her way upward, inch by inch. And she loved being alone up there, that feeling of total self-reliance. If she failed, she had no one to blame but herself.

Abby had never even seen a real mountain with her own eyes, much less tried to climb one. So for now, the wall would have to do. And as she walked toward her second-period class, she replayed every step and each grip of today's ascent, running through it like a slow-motion movie in her head.

She gave it her full attention for two reasons. First, she wanted to make a better climb next time—a perfect climb. And second, thinking about the wall was much more fun than dreading all the math and science and reading and social studies she was going to have to endure for the next six hours. After first-period gym class, Abby felt like the rest of the school day was zero fun— like a winter with no snow. Or a summer without sunshine. And these days, she was under a ton of extra pressure.

Because the truth was, Abby had never been a very good student. And during the first half of sixth grade, her academic problems had gone from bad to worse.

And then, about two weeks ago in February, her problems had moved beyond worse—all the way to rotten.

CHAPTER 3

# WORST CASE

Abby enjoyed a number of things about
school. She loved the noise and energy
on her bus every morning, and she
always sat with her friend Mariah way in the back
with the other sixth graders. She loved hanging out with her friends in the hallways, and she
was very proud of the incredible mess inside her
locker. On most days she even liked the food
in the cafe-teria, and when they served grilled
cheese with a half cup of sweet canned pears, she
always went back for seconds. She loved afternoon recess, loved art class and music class, and
absolutely adored gym class, especially on the
days when she got to climb.

Really, the only problem Abby had with

school was all that schoolwork. She didn't like it, and she never had. She was a decent reader, she was okay at math, and she was plenty smart. It wasn't that she couldn't do the work. She just didn't *like* doing it.

And most of the time, she didn't see the point. For example, how many times was some math teacher going to make her prove that she really did know how to add and subtract and multiply and divide? Enough, already.

And if she knew how to write a decent sentence with a subject and a verb, and if she always remembered to put a capital letter at the beginning and a punctuation mark at the end, then why did she have to suffer through all those endless writing exercises? It wasn't like she had plans to get a job writing for a newspaper or something.

Plus, she knew the names of all fifty states, and she knew where they were on the map, and she also knew the names of all the capital cities. Like Helena, Montana. And she knew how to find all seven continents on a globe, knew the beginning and ending dates for lots of important wars, knew the first sentence of the preamble to the Declaration of Independence by heart, and she could recite almost half of Lincoln's Gettysburg

Address. She even knew the names of the five countries that are permanent members of the United Nations Security Council. So why did she have to keep reading and reading those huge, thick social studies books every single year?

Because Abby didn't like being cooped up in her room or the library, sitting at a desk with her nose in some book or her fingers tapping on a keyboard. She wanted more hands-on experience with rock climbing, wanted to learn more about tying knots and rappelling, wanted to learn about all the technical gear like cams and pitons and pulleys. And especially, she wanted to be outside.

She wanted to be getting her boots muddy in the woods and fields behind her house. She wanted to be sharpening her skill with the bow and arrows she had made. She wanted to be fixing up the shelter she'd started to build in the huge oak tree that had blown over during a storm last summer. Schoolwork—and especially homework—felt like an interruption, something that kept her from doing all the things she liked best. Even though her parents kept after her, she never really gave her schoolwork much attention or effort. So during the first half of the year

Abby's grades, which had never been great, slid a little lower.

In the back of her mind, Abby knew she was getting near some kind of danger point. So when the school guidance counselor sent a note and called her out of gym class one morning in February, she wasn't that surprised. She'd had a talk with Mrs. Carmody about her schoolwork during fourth grade, and two talks during fifth grade. As she walked through the office and into the guidance center, she had a pretty good idea about what to expect.

"Hi, Mrs. Carmody. You wanted to see me?"

"Yes, Abby. Let's sit over at the table."

Abby saw that the table had already been set with two places, sort of like for a meal—one place with a white business-size envelope, and the other with a thick green file folder. Mrs. Carmody took the chair in front of the folder, and as Abby sat, she saw that the white envelope had her name on it.

She picked it up and said, "Am I supposed to read this?"

Mrs. Carmody said, "Yes, but let's talk a little first, all right?" The counselor paused a moment. "Your academic teachers have asked me to tell you and your parents that they think it might be best if you repeat sixth grade next year. And I've looked over your records, and I think they're right. That's what that letter is about. Now, you can be the one to tell your mom and dad about this, or if you'd like, I can give them a phone call today to let them know the letter is on its way. I've mailed it to them, but I wanted to talk to you so it wouldn't come as a total surprise. So, can I answer any questions for you?"

Abby's mouth was suddenly so dry that her tongue felt as if it had stuck to her teeth. She stared at Mrs. Carmody, and for almost five seconds it was like someone had pushed the pause button for the entire universe. She whispered, "I'm gonna be . . . left back?"

The counselor nodded. "That is what we're recommending. Junior high school is hard enough all by itself, without having to catch up on basic academics. I'm sure you can understand that. We've had some experience with other students, and another year here will really be a big help to you, especially later on."

Abby kept staring. "But, *left back*? I can't do that. I mean . . . I can't do that."

"I know it's a lot to take in all at once like this,

but just take a deep breath or two, and remember that what we want to do here is what's best for you. That's all. Can I get you a drink of water?"

Abby shook her head.

"Do you want to talk about this?"

She shook her head again and said, "I . . . I don't know what to say about it. I mean, it's like you said. A lot to take in."

"Well, it is, and I understand that, I really do. But I want you to remember that we want whatever's best for you. So, for now, you should probably go on back to class, and just think about it, all right? And if you want to talk to me again later today, here's a permission note you can use anytime." She slid a slip of paper across the table to Abby. "And let me know if you'd like me to be the one to tell your mom and dad, all right?"

Abby took the permission note and put it into the white envelope. As she stood up, Mrs. Carmody said, "Everything's going to work out, Abby. You'll see. So I'll talk to you later."

Abby nodded and said, "Okay." She tried to smile a little, but her face wasn't working. She walked through the office, and then out the door and along the fourth-grade hallway back toward the gym.

Several of the fourth-grade classroom doors

were open, and the different sounds spilled out into the air around her—kids reading aloud, a teacher leading a math class, a video on space exploration. But all Abby could hear was her own voice: *I'm gonna get left back.*

When she went into the gym, a furious game of dodgeball was under way, so she walked over to where her friend Mariah was sitting against the wall. Mariah hated dodgeball, and she always got hit on purpose right away.

Mariah said, "What was that about?"

"Nothing much."

Mariah turned and took a good look into her friend's face. "Are you sick or something? You look terrible."

"I'm fine," Abby said.

But that was a lie.


By the end of school on that Tuesday in February, Abby had bounced back a little. She had read the letter carefully, she had looked at the problem, and she had looked at herself. And then she had made some decisions, and she had also taken a few first steps to try to deal with this new situation.

One of her decisions had been to ask Mrs. Carmody not to call her parents. She wanted to break the bad news to them herself. This had seemed like a good idea at about two thirty in the afternoon. But around seven o'clock that evening, Abby was wishing she had gotten Mrs. Carmody's phone number.

It took every bit of courage she had, but when all three of them were in the kitchen after dinner, she managed to say, "Hey, Mom, Dad? I've got to talk to you about something—a problem. It's . . . pretty bad. Like, it's *really* bad."

Abby saw her mom's cheeks go pale as she quickly took a chair at the kitchen table. And as her dad put a bowl on the counter and laid down the dish towel, his face looked like he'd just hit his thumb with a hammer.

Abby took the white envelope out of her back pocket, unfolded it, and handed it to her mom. "It's about my grades."

"Oh . . . grades," her dad said. "That's good—I mean, it's not good. It's just good that it's not something else."

Her mom seemed relieved too as she took the envelope and pulled out a blue sheet of paper. And Abby thought, *What did they think the problem was gonna be?* But that thought would have to wait for later.

Her dad walked around the table and read over his wife's shoulder.

Abby said, "I . . . I just got that letter this morning, from the school counselor. And you're going to get it in the mail, probably tomorrow. But I wanted to tell you about it myself first. And I know that what the letter says sounds bad. But I'm already working on a plan, starting tomorrow—I mean, starting tonight, like, right now. Really. And I don't think it's too late to fix things. It's not."

"'Fix things'?" her dad said. Abby knew that tone of voice, and she braced herself. Whatever other problems her dad had imagined a moment ago, those were gone. And now he had fastened onto this one like a bulldog. "The school year is more than half gone, and your teachers are telling us that you are probably going to have to repeat sixth grade, and you think there's some kind of a quick fix? It doesn't work like that, Abby."

"I can go to summer school, if I have to," said Abby. "I mean, the letter's just a warning, right? And this is only February. It's not like it's completely going to happen."

Her mom looked down and read out loud. "'As you were informed in the January grade report,

Abby's work in math, science, reading, and social studies has been below grade level standards. She is still seriously behind in her work, and recent test scores have been low. It is very likely that she will need to repeat grade six.'"

Abby said, "See? It says 'very likely.' So it's not for sure. It's not."

"Even if you made some big changes," said her dad, "and I mean *huge* changes, that still might not be enough. Because this has been coming for a long time. This is a real mess."

"I know," she said, "and I'm going to work harder, a *lot* harder. I will, I promise. Starting right away. And before I left school today, I asked Mrs. Cooper and Mrs. Beckland to meet with me tomorrow morning. I'll find out what I have to do so I don't get left back. And I'm going to do everything I can. I promise."

"Well, we'll be talking to your teachers too," her mom said. "But I have to say I'm disappointed. When we got that warning on your last report card, you said you were going to make changes—you promised then, too, remember? Which is why I wasn't looking over your shoulder every second. And I'm sorry we didn't keep a closer eye on you. And now it might be too late. We should have been checking your work every day."

"Which is a mistake we won't make again," her dad added. "If you weren't able to do the work, and you actually needed more time to understand everything, that would be fine. But you shouldn't have to repeat a grade, Abby. There's no good reason for it. We'll help as much as we can right now, but you're the one who has to dig in and do the kind of work you're capable of. Right?"

Abby nodded. "Right."

"And," he went on, "even if there's no way to bring your grades up enough to get promoted this year, the way you treat your schoolwork has *got* to change anyway, starting right here, right now. Agreed?"

"Yes," Abby said. "Agreed."

"Now," her mom said, "show me what you have to do for tomorrow. Any tests coming up this week? Any projects due?"

For the next two hours Abby sat at the kitchen table and did her homework under the watchful eye of her mom. She read a chapter in her social studies book, then wrote out the answers to the questions at the end. She practiced her spelling words, did a grammar worksheet, memorized the symbols of ten elements in the periodic table, and finished all of the odd-numbered problems on page 177 of her math book.

And that took care of Wednesday's work. Which left time for a half hour of TV, a quick cell phone chat with Mariah, a snack, and a good-night kiss from her mom and dad.

As she went up the stairs to get ready for bed, Abby realized that this was the first time all year that she had finished every bit of her homework. It felt great to be completely prepared for the next day. Wednesday was going to be a breeze.

But as she put her head on her pillow that Tuesday night, the fears began to whisper inside her head:

*You think just because you did all your homework one night, they're going to let you go on to seventh grade? Ha! You are so stupid!*

*Face it: You're a lousy student. You've never been a good student, and you never will be. So get used to it. You're gonna flunk sixth grade, and next year you'll have to do this same boring stuff all over again.*

*And all your friends will be looking back at you from junior high. And they're gonna laugh and point at you. And all the moms are gonna wag their fingers* and say, *"Better study hard, or you'll get left back—just like Abby Carson."*

She sat straight up in bed, her heart thumping, her face burning, her fists clenched. And right out loud she said, "I am *not* going to be left back. I'll work really hard, and my mom and dad will help me, and so will my teachers. I'm *going* to junior high school next year. And I am *not* stupid!"

# CHAPTER 4

# STEEP CLIMB

When Abby's bus arrived at school on that Wednesday in February—the day after the academic warning letter—she got off, walked to the front doors, told the teacher on duty that she had a meeting in room 133, and then headed for the sixth-grade wing.

The halls were mostly empty and quiet. It was a long walk, so Abby had time to think about how she did *not* want to be taking this same walk in September as a sixth grader—for the second year in a row.

The door of room 133 was closed, so Abby knocked, and a voice called out, "Come in."

She opened the door, and Mrs. Cooper said, "Good morning, Abby. Come have a seat."

There was no smile on her face, no smile in her voice. And Abby saw the grade book, lying open on the desk.

Mrs. Cooper was Abby's math and science teacher, and this was her classroom. She was sitting behind her desk, and there were two chairs in front of it. Mrs. Beckland, who taught language arts and social studies, was already sitting in one of them.

The moment Abby sat down, she blurted out, "I'm going to do everything I can so I don't get left back, and I'm sorry I haven't been working very much, and I'm going to do a lot better. So I want you to tell me what I have to do." She paused, and then remembered to say, "Please."

"Well, we certainly want to help you in every way we can, Abby," said Mrs. Cooper. "But you're in a tough spot right now." She put one finger on her grade book and moved it sideways across the page, following it with her eyes. She shook her head and said, "Things look pretty bad in science. And also in math."

Mrs. Beckland had her grade book open too. She nodded and said, "And it's not good in language arts or social studies, either. You would need very high marks on all the rest of your tests and quizzes to get promoted to seventh grade."

Abby leaned forward in her chair and said, "But if I *do* get really good grades from now on, that means I'd be okay, right?"

Mrs. Beckland said, "I don't know if I can promise that, Abby. I don't want to discourage you, but your grade average would have to come up a long way from where it is now. And, of course, you would also need to do well when you take the Illinois achievement tests."

Abby said, "I could go to summer school, too, couldn't I? To bring up my grades?"

"Our district doesn't have academic summer school for sixth graders," said Mrs. Cooper. "So no, that's not an option." Still no smile, no warmth at all from the math lady.

Abby felt like her grip on junior high school was slipping. She looked from one teacher's face to the other, and then locked onto Mrs. Beckland's eyes, pleading. "There must be something I could do. To be sure that I get promoted. Isn't there something?"

Mrs. Beckland looked from Abby's face to Mrs. Cooper's. And Mrs. Beckland said, "Excuse us a moment."

And both teachers stood up and walked out of the room, pulling the door shut behind them.

Abby turned, and she saw Mrs. Cooper's back through the glass panel of the door, and she heard a quiet murmur as the teachers talked.

And she thought, *I know they can help me. If they want to. And I'm sure they want to. Because they're both nice . . . kind of.* Abby thought another second. *And besides, I bet they don't really want me hanging around here again next year.*

A minute later both teachers walked back in and sat down.

Mrs. Beckland said, "To be promoted to seventh grade, you would have to do three things. First, you would have to do all your homework every day from now on, in every subject."

Abby nodded and said, "I could do that . . . I mean, I will. I *will* do that."

Mrs. Cooper said, "And second, you're going to need to get at least a strong B, that's eighty-five percent or better, on all your tests and quizzes from now on, in every subject."

Abby nodded again. "If I work really hard, I could do that. And I will."

Mrs. Beckland said, "And finally, since your language arts and social studies grades are worse than your math and science grades, you would also have to do a special assignment for me, a project.

For extra credit. Are you willing to do that?"

The thought of even more schoolwork was horrible, but Abby managed to smile and say, "Sure . . . but, like, what kind of project?"

"I've got a number of different assignments," she said, "and you would have to pick one. And you'd have to do a great job to get the credit—plus keep up with all your regular work. It won't be easy."

"But if it means I'll get promoted," Abby said, "then I'll do whatever I have to, I really will. And I'll do a good job on everything, from now on. And I've already started, because I did all my homework for today."

Mrs. Beckland said, "All right then. I'll make up an academic contract. And Mrs. Cooper and I will sign it, and you'll sign it, and your parents will sign it. And then it will be up to you to do the work."

"And I know you can," said Mrs. Cooper, and she gave Abby a thin smile, not exactly warm, but sincere.

Mrs. Beckland stood up and said, "Now let's go next door so you can pick out your project. Because you'll need to get started on it right away."

Abby got up from her chair and went toward

the doorway, but then stopped and turned around. "Thanks, Mrs. Cooper."

The math teacher smiled again, a few degrees warmer. "You're welcome, Abby. See you later."

As Abby followed Mrs. Beckland out of the math room, she tried to keep a strong, confident look on her face. But walking along the hallway, her eyebrows scrunched together, and she began biting her lower lip the way she did when she watched a horror movie.

And she thought, *I actually have to get a B or better on every test and quiz? And never miss a homework assignment? For the rest of the year? How is that even possible?*

Because ever since third grade, when that first batch of letters appeared on her report card, Abby had never been a solid B student. More like a shaky C student. And sometimes, a D student. And now it was like she had to go from flunking out to being on the honor roll—instantly. And if she couldn't, then next year would be déjà vu— sixth grade all over again.

She thought, *For the next four and half months my life is gonna be nothing but homework, quizzes, and tests. Plus the extra-credit project. So basically . . . I'm dead.*

# CHAPTER 5

# THE PROJECT

Abby followed Mrs. Beckland into room 131 and watched as she opened a cabinet and took down a large shoe box from the top shelf. It was covered with red construction paper, and there was a hole in the lid about as big as a TV remote. On the long side of the box, printed in neat black letters, were two words: EXTRA CREDIT.

"How come I've never seen that before?" Abby asked.

"Because I'd rather have kids doing a good job on all their regular assignments instead of relying on last-minute bailouts. But there are always exceptional cases." Mrs. Beckland gave the box a few good shakes and said, "Here's the way this works. I've got about ten different assignments in this box, each one written on a folded piece of paper. You reach in and pull one out, and *that's* the project you have to do—no second choices, no backsies." She held the box in front of Abby. "So, pick one."

Abby put her hand into the box, and groped around until she had hold of a piece of paper. Then she let go of that one, and found another and started to pull her hand out. But then she let go of that paper too, and reached over into a corner, grabbed a third piece, and pulled it out.

Mrs. Beckland said, "Go ahead and read it out loud."

Abby unfolded the paper and her voice filled the empty classroom: "Project Pen Pal. Number one: Your teacher will help you find the name and address of a school in another part of the world, somewhere with a culture different from yours.

"Number two: You will write a letter and ask a student at this other school to become your pen pal.

"Number three: Using copies of the letters you send, plus the letters you receive, you will make a bulletin board display in the classroom.

You will update your display as often as there are new letters.

"Number four: When you have written and received at least four letters, you will give an oral report to the class about what you have learned from this experience."

That was the whole assignment, and after she finished reading it aloud, Abby read it again silently.

Mrs. Beckland said, "So, what do you think?"

"Sounds like a lot of work, a lot of writing . . . but sort of fun, too," she added quickly. "And you're going to help me find a school I can write to?"

The teacher nodded. "I've got some good contacts—e-mail connections with a teacher in Jakarta, Indonesia; with a school administrator in Kabul, Afghanistan; and with a professor in Beijing, China. Any of those places sound interesting to you?"

"I . . . I don't know," said Abby. She didn't know a thing about those places, except that the Olympics had been in Beijing. Then, a thought: "But . . . are there mountains there, in those places? *Big* mountains?"

Mrs. Beckland said, "Take a look at a globe and decide for yourself."

There were three globes on a table by the windows: a political globe that showed all the countries of the world in different colors; a historical globe that showed the different countries of the world in the year 1800; and a raised-relief globe with a textured surface that showed mountain ranges, river valleys, ocean trenches, and other physical features of the Earth.

The teacher pointed at the raised-relief globe. "All right, start by finding Australia." Abby turned the globe and put her finger on it.

"Now, to the north and west of Australia, that long arc of islands? That's part of Indonesia, and right there on Java, that's the capital city, Jakarta."

Abby moved her fingers across the area. "Not very mountainous."

Her teacher nodded. "That's because it's not very high above sea level—which is true about a lot of islands. Now, can you find Beijing?"

Abby traced her finger northward from Jakarta, across the South China Sea to Hong Kong, followed the coastline north past the island of Taiwan, then moved inland from Shanghai. "There," she said. "Beijing."

"Any mountains?"

Abby shook her head. "Pretty flat."

"Okay," Mrs. Beckland said, "move south and west from Beijing toward India."

Abby did, and when she got close to India, she said, "Mountains—*huge* ones."

"Right. Which ones are they?"

Abby read. "'The Himalayas'—that's where Mount Everest is."

"Right. Now follow the mountains north and west—good . . . stop. That's the country of Pakistan. And if you move straight west from there, you'll come to Afghanistan, and its capital."

Abby spelled it out. "K-a-b-u-l . . . How is it pronounced?"

"Just the way it looks. It's a short *A* sound, with the accent on the first syllable: KA-bul. How does the land seem there—flat or mountainous?"

Abby said, "Well, it's not like the Himalayas, but it's nowhere near as flat as Beijing or Java."

"Right," her teacher said, "and all those bumps and ridges north of Kabul? Those are the Hindu Kush mountains, very steep and rugged."

Abby said, "Then I want to find a pen pal around that part of Afghanistan."

Mrs. Beckland nodded. "All right. And I think

that's a good choice. I'll try to get you the address you need before the end of the day tomorrow."

And just two days later, Abby had written and mailed her first letter to Afghanistan—the letter in the green envelope. The letter that arrived during the second week of March at a village school in the hills above Kabul.

# CHAPTER 6

# STUCK BETWEEN

Will you read the letter this time? Will you? Pleeease?"

Sadeed shook his head. "No. And stop whining. If you don't practice reading English, you'll never get better at it. And don't touch that writing paper again or I'm going to take you outside and push your face in some snow. Now begin reading. And look carefully at each word before you say it this time."

Sadeed knew he was being tough on Amira, but all this? It was too much to ask of any self-respecting boy, especially one who would be twelve in four short months.

The brother and sister sat side by side on the charpoy, a low, four-legged bed that the family used as a couch. They were in the central room, one of four in the small stone and mud brick house just off the main street near the western edge of the village. This room was the warmest one during the winter because the kitchen was at the far end. The evening meal wouldn't be until after the bazaar closed and evening prayers ended, but the small charcoal cookstove was already lit, partly for warmth. Their mother had come home from her work at the sewing co-op to heat up some rice for the children's lunch, and now she stood at a wooden table by the stove, cutting chunks of lamb, onions, and lemon slices to make a stew for dinner.

Sadeed gritted his teeth as Amira began to read the letter aloud for the second time, still stumbling over the simplest words. But he couldn't really blame her. First of all, the handwriting in this letter was sloppy. The words had been written with a dull pencil on a piece of lined paper with a ragged edge. English was a hard language anyway, and remembering that the sentences had to be read from left to right was difficult. Plus, he reminded himself that Amira was almost two years younger than he was.

Still, it was painful to listen to her read.

"Dear Pen Pal,

My name is Abby Carson, and I live in the town of Linsdale in the state of Illinois in the United States of America. Illinois is sort of in the middle of our country. It is flat farmland all around here—almost completely flat. What does it look like where you live? Can you see any mountains?

The truth is, I'm writing this letter as a special school assignment. And I guess this letter might make some extra work for you, too—whoever you are. And I say that because until you write back, I won't know who I'm actually writing to. But the more I think about how this letter is going to travel all the way to Afghanistan, it's sort of amazing. We hear about your country in the news here in America, mostly about how there has been so much fighting. Is there fighting around where you live? I hope not."

As his sister continued to struggle with each word, Sadeed thought back to what his teacher had said to him at noon as he and the other morning students were dismissed from school for the day.

"Sadeed, I'm giving you this task because I have faith in you. You will do a fine job. And I know you will make our village proud . . . you and your sister, I mean. I have spoken to her. She will be writing to a student in America. But not alone. Amira will sign the letter, because the American is a girl, and that is the most proper way, to have one girl writing to another. And Amira has promised she will not talk to others about how you are helping her to write. But you will watch to be sure Amira writes well. And that she says interesting things, good things. And now I give the letter to you, for safekeeping. Do you understand?"

"Yes, sir," Sadeed said, remembering to look surprised about the whole arrangement as he took the letter.

But, of course, he had been expecting this, because of what he'd overheard at Akbar Khan's compound. And as he accepted the letter, he noticed how his teacher gave no hint that the village elders had insisted he take this approach. He thought, *It must be hard to have so many masters.*

Not that Sadeed had ever imagined that his teacher had an easy job. Mahmood was the only teacher for more than a hundred boys and girls. The village school had just one room, and the children in grades one through six attended as one large group in the morning. In the afternoon the older students attended, with a movable partition down the center of the room, boys on the right, girls on the left.

Sadeed was able to tolerate the younger students in the morning class with him, but just barely. *Really,* he thought, *Mahmood should make me his assistant for the rest of this year.* Because he saw so clearly how skillful Mahmood was at keeping different groups of kids working on different levels at the same time. *I could do that,* he thought. *At least the man has the good sense to make sure that advanced sixth-grade students like me have plenty of challenging work. So that's good.* Sadeed was especially glad that Mahmood allowed him to borrow from his small library of English-language books. He had read all of them except *Great Expectations,* a very long British novel. *I expect I shall read that book soon—shouldn't take me more than a few days.*

Amira stopped reading, which snapped Sadeed back to the present moment.

"What?" he said. "Why did you stop?"

"Because you're not even listening to me," she said, pushing out her lower lip.

"I can hear you just fine," he lied, "and you're doing a good job. So keep reading, and hurry it up a little."

Amira heaved a sigh and resumed reading, even slower than before.

> "So anyway, I hope you tell me
> something about yourself when you
> write back. And maybe tell me about
> your family. And also tell me what
> it's like where you live, and what you
> look like. And if you have a picture
> to send me, that would be fun to
> see."

Sadeed's mind drifted back again to the talk with his teacher. The envelope he had been given was a brilliant green color, like an apple in July. Two pink paper butterflies were pasted on the front, one on either side of the address. Every other letter Sadeed had seen in his life had looked serious, important. Some had been pale blue airmail envelopes, others dark brown or white, loaded up with official stickers and postmarks and stamps. This letter was clearly not serious at all. And there were only three stamps on the envelope, each one a small picture of an American flag.

Along with the letter Mahmood had also given him a new pencil, a dozen sheets of bright white paper, and five envelopes with official international airmail stamps on each one. Sadeed had carefully tucked everything but the pencil between the pages of his school notebook.

His teacher said, "The bus that comes from Kabul twice each week? The driver will carry the letter back to a post office. It is all arranged. So the letter must be ready by tomorrow afternoon. I'm sorry it must be done so quickly, but it cannot be helped. Can you and your sister prepare a letter that soon?"

Again Sadeed had said, "Yes, sir," and nodded respectfully.

As Sadeed had left the school, his friend Najeeb was waiting outside, his sheepskin collar pulled up high against the biting wind. "What did your best friend want to tell you? Are you being honored again? Or did he ask if he could shine your shoes for you?"

Sadeed shoved Najeeb so that he almost stepped into a pile of goat droppings. "It was just about some work I have to do, nothing a fool like you would understand."

As he talked, he kept a tight grip on his school notebook. If his friends ever found out that he had been given a silly green envelope containing a letter from a girl, he would be teased and taunted for the rest of his life.

As Amira neared the end of the American girl's letter, Sadeed wished he'd been able to avoid this task somehow.

Because now he had no choice but to help his sister. In truth, he would have to practically write a letter for her. And then she would sign it. And then the letter would be sent to this girl in America. And then *she* would probably write back again.

So he would be stuck between two girls for weeks, maybe months, forced to listen in to their pointless chitchat—could anything be worse? What a terrible waste of time and paper and stamps.

And now his sister was supposed to write a perfect letter? In one afternoon? In English? It would be easier teaching a dog to drive a motorbike.

Amira read the last few sentences.

"I hope you write back soon, because
if I don't get enough letters from
you, then I won't get a good grade
on this project. And I really need a
good grade. Are you a good student?
I hope so.
Thanks for reading this, and I'll be
watching for your first letter to me.


Sincerely, your American pen pal,
Abby Carson"

Sadeed looked again at the photograph that had
come in the envelope. The girl wasn't even facing toward the camera. She was clinging to a gray
wall that was covered with bumps, holding on the
way a spider does, her arms and legs spread wide.
A rope hanging from above went to a wide belt at
her waist. Her head was uncovered, and her light
brown hair was short, not even to her shoulders.
She wore red trousers with the word LIONS written
along the outside of the leg. She had black shoes on
her feet, and she wore a yellow T-shirt. Her arms
looked thin. Also strong, for a girl. The skin of her

arms and face was pale. She was looking upward, and the expression on her face was stern, almost angry.

And this spider girl was the cause of his problem, the creator of all this extra work. Which seemed so pointless. And which also seemed false, to pretend that Amira would be answering the letter on her own.

However, Sadeed had made a promise to his teacher, and a man must keep his word.

"All right," he said, "the pencil is sharp, and now I want you to use your best writing. In English. First think, then tell me the word you are going to write, and how it is spelled. In English. And then write the word on the paper. Do you understand?"

Amira nodded. "Of course I understand. And stop talking to me like I'm a baby."

So the work began.

# CHAPTER 7

# WORD FOR WORD

Slowly, patiently, Sadeed tried to coax a sensible letter out of his sister, one word, one sentence at a time. After three minutes she had written the date. It took another five minutes for her to write the words "Dear Abby in America."

And ten minutes later, when she was struggling to write the word "village," Sadeed could not stand it one second longer.

"Your head is full of rocks—I give up!" he shouted. And he grabbed the paper from his sister and tore it to shreds.

Amira burst into tears.

From the kitchen at the end of the room, their mother stopped kneading a large lump of dough.

She looked at Sadeed. She didn't scold, but he saw her frown.

He took a deep breath. Then another.

And then he said, "Look, don't cry, Amira. I shouldn't have yelled at you." And thinking fast, he added, "Really, it's not your fault. You just don't know English well enough to do this. You barely know how to shape the letters correctly, much less spell all the words and get the grammar right. It's a hard language."

Sadeed had meant that to comfort her, but Amira wailed even louder. Between sobs, she said, "The teacher . . . is going to think . . . I'm *stupid* . . . just like you do!"

"I don't think that," he said, "and neither does the teacher." He gave her an awkward pat on the shoulder. "Just stop crying, okay? Because I have an idea, and you're really going to like it. Ready?"

She looked up at him, and the tears on her cheeks made him feel terrible.

"Here," he said, gently taking the pencil from her. He opened to a fresh page in his school notebook. "You just tell me what you want to say to this girl. Talk to me in Dari, and I'll write it in my notebook first, and then later I'll copy it onto the good paper. In English. And then you can sign your name to it. I'll be like a letter writer sitting on his stool at the bazaar, and you'll be the customer, telling me what to write."

Amira dried her eyes with the edge of the dark blue scarf that covered her head and shoulders. She sniffed, and blinked, and looked up at him. "And you'll write exactly what I say?"

"I will." Sadeed nodded, beginning to feel impatient again. "So begin telling me. Right now. We can't take the whole day with this, all right? Tell me what to write." Sadeed wanted to get this over with and then go put in a few hours at his afternoon job.

So Amira began to dictate her letter.

"Dear Abby in America,
    I am Amira. I am ten and a half years old.
    I live in a village called Bahar-Lan. It is about a hundred and twenty kilometers north of Kabul. We still have some snow on the ground here, but the days are sometimes warmer now. The snow will not be all gone until at least another two months. At night it is still cold.

I am in the fourth grade at
our school. I study very hard. A
lot of the other girls in our village
go to school also, and I am glad
that my father permits it. I love
to read, and I am getting better
at writing. I am studying English
also.

I have a mother and a father and
a brother. My uncle and his wife
also live with us in our house. But
soon he will have his own home.
I will be sad when they move, but
there will be more room. So that
will be good.

Thank you for the photograph. All
I can see is that your hair is pale and
that you are wearing a yellow shirt
and red pants. Why is there a wall of
rock with a roof above it? I do not
understand that.

I haven't got a picture I can send
back to you, as we do not have a
camera. But a man who lives near us
owns one, and maybe I can ask for
his help."

Amira kept talking for several more minutes, non-stop. Sadeed was actually quite impressed that his sister was able to speak a letter out loud this way and have most of it make perfect sense. When she finally ran out of things to say, she finished with,

"Abby, I thank you very much for
writing to me. And I hope my
letter finds you and your family in
fine health, God-be-willing.

Your friend in Afghanistan,
Amira Bayat"

As promised, Sadeed had written down exactly what she said, word for word. He showed his notebook to her, and she smiled and said, "Thank you, Mr. Letter Writer."

And then Amira hopped off the charpoy and went to help her mother get ready to carry their flatbread dough to the oven at the village baking co-op.

Before they were out the door, Sadeed had already begun translating Amira's letter into English. He made a rough draft on a new page in his note-book, and then used his neatest handwriting and copied the words over onto a fresh piece of white paper. In fifteen minutes he had filled one side of a sheet. After ten minutes more he had covered half the other side, and that was it. The letter was ready for Amira's signature.

Sadeed put all the papers away, carefully closed up his notebook, grabbed his hat and coat, and then dashed out the door to go to his father's shop. Some new shipments of wheat flour, lentils, and rice were supposed to arrive, and he knew he'd be needed to help his father and his uncle stack the heavy sacks.

He set off at a brisk walk. It was mostly uphill to the bazaar, more than half a kilometer along the main road that ran through the center of town.

Sadeed heard the roar of a truck as it climbed the steep grade toward the village, but the sound was an echo from the far side of the marketplace, where the roadway got wider. Near his house, the oncoming traffic was mostly women and girls walking home from the bazaar with their parcels and bags of food. Up ahead he saw people headed the same way he was: a herdsman carrying a bundle of wool, a woman with two sacks of charcoal hanging from the yoke across her shoulders, a boy leading a donkey with a bundle of carpets tied to

the pack saddle. Sadeed noticed everything, and he nodded and smiled when neighbors greeted him, but his mind was elsewhere, still distracted by this letter-writing business.

Amira's sudden outburst of tears had been a surprise. She really wanted to do a good job on the letter, wanted to be proud of her work. *I would want to do a good job too, of course,* he thought. *But I'd never start crying about it.* Which made him think about how different he was from his sister, and from girls in general. That thought bounced around his mind for several minutes. Girls were a great mystery.

As he neared the bazaar, the dirt street widened into the central market area. The permanent stalls on both sides of the street had been built so that the doorways were above the level of the roadway, and running along in front of each row of shops was a knee-high platform of rocks and dirt, something like a porch. The common roof that ran above the stalls extended out over the raised porch area, and this gave the shopkeepers and their goods a little shelter from the weather. Stout wooden doors, two for each shop, were propped open for business, locked and bolted shut each night.

At this time of year the market always seemed

dull and slow to Sadeed. The permanent stalls were the only places doing business. He loved the bazaar best from late spring through the fall, when the whole market area would be packed from morning to night with vendors selling from pushcarts, from small wagons, from baskets, or from cloths spread out over the ground. Potatoes, fruit, spices, shoes, tools, books, charcoal, kerosene, clothing, leather, cloth, cookware, meat, poultry, portable radios, lumber, woodstoves, bicycles, tea—almost anything was available when the bazaar was in full session.

"Are you hungry, boy?" Sadeed was only five or six stalls away from his father's, and the man calling to him was a food vendor named Rafi. He was holding out a kebab. "Stupid question—boys are always hungry. Here, take it." He winked and said, "I'll put this on your father's account."

Sadeed grinned and accepted the short wooden skewer of roasted chunks of lamb and red peppers. "Mmm—smells delicious. Thank you."

"Just come back and spend money someday," the man said. "And tell the people you meet where you got that."

As he wolfed down his first bite of grilled meat, Sadeed got a clear look at his afternoon's work.

His father's shop was two stalls wide. One was used mostly for storage, which left the floor area of the other stall uncluttered so customers could step inside and have their purchases weighed on the scale hanging from the ceiling. And there on the porch in front of the storage stall, forty or fifty bags of grain and flour were piled up, some delivered from Kabul by truck, others no doubt brought by donkey or oxcart from local mills and grain growers. Sadeed wished he'd been around to hear the haggling over the prices—his father was a master at striking a good deal.

"Finally come to work, have you, boy? And I see you've brought me a snack." His father didn't smile, but Sadeed knew he was joking. Nodding at the stack of bags, his father said, "Well, you'd better eat all that yourself. You'll need your strength."

For the next hour and a half, Sadeed and his uncle Asif worked side by side, first clearing out the storeroom, and then stacking the newest sacks farthest away from the door. It was important to sell the older flour and grain first, so that nothing would spoil.

As he worked, Sadeed kept thinking about Amira's letter. And about that girl hanging on the wall like a spider. And he realized that Amira hadn't answered the girl's question about the mountains. And Amira hadn't really told the American girl much about her family, either. *I could have written a much more interesting letter,* he thought. He heaved a twenty-kilo bag of flour onto the top of a stack. *But it's got nothing to do with me.* And he resolved not to think about that letter again.

A few minutes before seven the next morning, Sadeed met his teacher at the door of the school building and handed him Amira's letter.

The envelope had not been sealed, and Mahmood said, "May I read this?"

Sadeed said, "Certainly."

Mahmood took the letter out and turned so that the morning sunlight poured onto the paper. He read it quickly, smiled, and said, "It's good. Thank you, Sadeed."

"You're welcome." He shifted his weight from one foot to the other.

The teacher said, "Is there something else?"

Sadeed pulled some papers from his notebook. "I . . . I rewrote Amira's letter last night. Because it seemed like there were questions Amira forgot to answer. So this is what I wrote."

Mahmood took the sheets of paper and began

to read. Again, he smiled. "This is excellent. Very good indeed. And did Amira like the changes you made?"

"She liked the ones I showed her. But she hasn't seen all the changes . . . not yet."

"But why did she sign her name at the end of your letter?"

Sadeed shrugged. "I asked her to, and she did. She signed both letters." He paused, then said, "So . . . which letter should go to America?"

Sadeed already knew the answer to this question. He had heard Mahmood speaking to the village council. He had said, "Should we accept less than the very best writing, the best spelling and grammar?"

But Mahmood said, "It should be the first one, I think, Amira's letter. But leave both of them with me, all right? Either way, a fine letter from our village will be on its way to America by dinnertime. Now let's go to class, shall we?"

And on a Thursday morning in the hills above Kabul, the school day began.

# CHAPTER 8

# HOUSE, BARN, FIELDS, WOODS

Eleven days later and more than seven thousand miles to the west, Abby Carson got off the school bus, walked the long driveway, and let herself in the back door of the old farmhouse where she had lived her entire life.

"Hi," she called. "I'm home."

No answer, which is what she had been hoping for.

Because that meant neither her mom nor her dad was home from work yet. And since it was a sunny Monday afternoon in late March, and since she had less than an hour of homework, Abby dumped her book bag just inside the door of the mudroom, kicked off her school sneakers, pulled on her hiking boots, grabbed her green backpack, and headed for the woods.

The green backpack contained a flashlight, a butane lighter, a compass, a pocket knife, a folding pull saw, a small hatchet, some good climbing rope, a couple hundred feet of nylon cord, a liter of water, a space blanket, a nylon poncho, a pencil, a notebook, and about a dozen energy bars. Abby headed straight north, crossed the winter-brown lawn, and as she stepped onto a path leading through the tangled undergrowth of the woods, she dug around in the pack, found what she wanted, and started munching on an oatmeal raisin bar.

After walking less than three minutes, all traces of civilization vanished, and she was alone in the woods. But actually, she was still in her own backyard, because her home sat on sixty-seven acres. The house, yard, barn, and pasture took up eight acres or so; forty acres was farmland; and the rest was woods.

Abby's mom was in charge of the house, and that made sense because it was the home where she had grown up. When Abby's grandparents had retired and moved to Arizona, her parents had decided to stay on at the family farm.

Abby's dad looked after the farmland, but not really. Brent Collins from a mile up the road did the real farming, and her father just checked up on him now and then when the price of corn or soybeans got interesting.

Abby's brother, Tom, had chosen the barn and the small pasture as his territory. He had built himself a clubhouse in the hayloft, and also raised sheep to show at the 4-H Tri-county Fair. Or at least, he used to. Since getting to high school, he had become more interested in computers than livestock.

And about the time she had turned eight years old, Abby had decided that the woods belonged to her. And she was sure that she'd gotten the best deal. She had explored every inch of the nineteen wooded acres, from the small stream at the northern boundary, to the road on the east, to the fence line on the west. She knew every briar patch, every vine strong enough to climb, every clump of poison oak. She knew where to find sassafras saplings, where to look for wild blackberries, and where to hunt for red-bellied mud snakes. She knew where the rabbits had their warren, knew the hollow trees where raccoons hibernated, knew the pines where the horned owl slept on spring afternoons.

Today she was headed toward her newest tree

house. It wasn't a regular tree house, because this particular oak lay on the forest floor. The tree had originally stood about eighty feet tall, with a trunk almost three feet in diameter. During a gusty thunderstorm last July, the tree had toppled, and its roots had pulled up a circle of earth fifteen feet across. That root clump held the base of the tree seven or eight feet off the ground, and the upper branches had kept the crown of the tree from falling flat against the earth. This left the main trunk slanted upward at an angle of about twenty degrees—sort of like the deck of a ship that had run up onto a reef. Abby used one of the largest branches like a ladder to climb from the ground up to the trunk, and then she could walk up the trunk like a gangplank into the mass of tangled branches.

It really wasn't much of a fort, not yet. Abby had chopped off a couple dozen branches, each about ten or twelve feet long, and had lashed them together to make a rough platform laid across the trunk in the tree's upper canopy. Another bunch of shorter branches angled up from one edge of the platform to a crossbeam she had tied in place. This made a simple lean-to, open to the east and closed to the west, which was the direction most of the wind came from. Smaller leafy branches layered into the lean-to roof kept out most of the snow and rain. A heap of evergreen branches from a nearby hemlock tree made a soft and springy place to sit.

It looked more like a gorilla's nest than a tree house, but it was more than twenty feet up and it was invisible from the ground. The leaves of the dying tree had turned brown by late September, but most of them had stayed in place all fall and winter, which provided good natural camouflage. Abby intended to make some serious improvements to the hideout during the coming summer.

Back in October, Abby had done some Internet research about how to make a bow and arrows, and that had led her to the *U.S. Army Survival Manual*, which she had downloaded onto the family-room computer. And following the step-by-step directions, she'd found a dead oak sapling, cut and shaped it carefully with her hatchet, and made herself a sturdy bow with a string made of nylon parachute cord. All fall she added to her stock of handmade arrows whenever she found a long, straight stick.

Since bow hunting involved walking around on the ground, she kept her bow and arrows wrapped in plastic and hidden in the leaves at the base of the fallen oak, instead of up in the lean-to. And today she was going to have some target practice. She imagined herself getting good enough with the bow to shoot a rabbit—except she knew she'd have to be starving before she could make herself do that.

Just as the toppled tree came into view, Abby's cell phone vibrated in her pocket. She didn't need to look at the display to know who it was.

"Hi, Dad."

"Hi, sweetheart—I meant to be home by now, but it got busy all of a sudden, and your mom works until five thirty today. Everything okay with you?"

"Sure, I'm fine."

"Well, I just wanted to—"

High above Abby, a solitary crow gave one sharp warning caw.

Her dad said, "You're not in the house."

"No, but I—"

"Abby, I don't want to hear it. Turn yourself around and go right back inside and get on your homework."

"But I just got out here, Dad. And I need to be outside—you always say fresh air is good for

me, right? And I'll go back in an hour, I promise. Because I don't have much homework at all tonight."

"You've got more homework than you think you do."

"What? What do you mean?"

"Well, the mail came early this morning, and there's a letter waiting on the kitchen counter. You probably ran right past it. It's from your pen pal."

"Cool!"

"Yes, 'cool,' but you're going to have to write a reply tonight, and that's going to take time. So I want you to get home right now."

"Can't I stay out for just half an hour?"

There was a pause. "Back inside in thirty minutes, all right?"

"Thirty minutes," Abby said.

"Promise?"

"Yes, I promise."

"Good. See you soon, sweetheart."

"Bye, Dad."

Abby smiled as she tucked the phone back into her pocket. She had just won an argument, sort of. And she had bought herself half an hour of free time in the woods.

However, eight minutes later she was standing in the kitchen.

Because her woods weren't going anywhere, and she'd been out there hundreds of times.

But never in her life had she gotten a letter from someone who lived in the mountains on the other side of the world.

# CHAPTER 9

# ABBY IN AMERICA

Abby stood at the kitchen counter, holding a letter with her name and address on it, looking at the strange writing on the airmail stamps.

She started to rip the envelope open, but then stopped. She found a paring knife and used it to slit along the top edge so she wouldn't rip any of the stamps on the front of the envelope.

She sat on a stool at the counter, pulled the paper out, unfolded it, and began reading.

Dear Abby in America,

My name is Amira Bayat. I am ten years old and I attend grade four at my school

HERE IN PANJSHIR PROVINCE. OUR VILLAGE IS CALLED BAHAR-LAN. IT IS ABOUT 120 KILOMETERS NORTH FROM KABUL, OUR CAPITAL CITY. IT IS NOT A GREAT DISTANCE, BUT IT IS A FIVE- OR SIX-HOUR DRIVE OVER BAD ROADS. I HAVE NEVER GONE THERE, BUT MY FATHER AND MY UNCLE ASIF HAVE MADE THIS TRIP MANY TIMES.

ABOUT YOUR MOUNTAIN QUESTION, THE ANSWER IS YES. FROM ANYWHERE IN MY VILLAGE THERE ARE MOUNTAINS TO SEE. AT NIGHT THIS TIME OF YEAR I CAN HEAR ICE AND SNOW SLIDING OFF THE STEEPEST PLACES, CRASHING DOWN TO THE VALLEYS BELOW. GOD HELP ANYONE WHO GETS IN THE WAY.

I AM IN A FAMILY OF FOUR PEOPLE. MY MOTHER WORKS AT HOME AND AT A SEWING GROUP WITH FIVE OTHER WOMEN. MY FATHER AND MY UNCLE HAVE A SHOP WHERE THEY SELL FLOUR AND RICE AND OTHER GRAIN AND SEED FOODS. AND I ALSO HAVE ONE BROTHER, SADEED. HE IS A FINE STUDENT IN GRADE SIX, OFTEN AT THE HEAD OF HIS CLASS. HE IS ALSO VERY STRONG. HE LIKES TO READ AND DRAW. HIS TEACHERS HAVE TOLD HIM THAT HE

HAS A GIFT FOR WRITING POEMS. BUT HE IS NOT CONCEITED. HE IS QUITE A NICE FELLOW. AND HE IS SUPERB AT FLYING KITES. HE HAS WON MANY OF THE KITE FIGHTS.

I SEE IN YOUR PHOTOGRAPH THAT YOU ARE CLIMBING ON A WALL OF STONE THAT IS INSIDE A BUILDING. IS THIS SOMETHING YOU DO OFTEN? WHY?

WE DO NOT HAVE A CAMERA, SO I CANNOT SEND A PHOTO. BUT I HAVE ASKED MY BROTHER TO MAKE SOME LITTLE DRAWINGS. DO YOU LIKE TO DRAW? DO YOU HAVE MANY BOOKS IN YOUR HOME? I KNOW AMERICA IS A VERY RICH COUNTRY. WE HAVE ONLY ONE BOOK AT HOME RIGHT NOW, A NOVEL THAT MY BROTHER HAS BORROWED FROM OUR TEACHER.

I USUALLY WRITE IN A LANGUAGE CALLED DARI, BUT I AM TRYING TO LEARN ENGLISH, TOO. AND MY BROTHER SAYS I WILL BE AN EXPERT IN ENGLISH ONE DAY, THE WAY HE IS.

NOT ALL OF THE GIRLS IN MY VILLAGE ARE ALLOWED TO GO TO SCHOOL. I LOVE TO READ AND STUDY AND LEARN, AND I AM GLAD MY FATHER PERMITS THIS. I HOPE TO ATTEND A UNIVERSITY ONE DAY AND BECOME A TEACHER.

OUR COUNTRY NEEDS MANY TEACHERS, AND I THINK I COULD BE A GOOD ONE.

IN YOUR LETTER YOU SAID THAT YOU HAD HEARD ABOUT A LOT OF FIGHTING IN MY COUNTRY. WHAT YOU HEARD IS TRUE. BUT IN OUR OWN VILLAGE, THERE HAS BEEN NO SHOOTING OR BOMBS OF ANY KIND FOR ALMOST HALF OF A YEAR. THAT IS GOOD. DURING THE WORST FIGHTING, I WAS ONLY A BABY. BUT MY BROTHER SADEED REMEMBERS THE SOUNDS OF BOMBS AND SHOOTING AND SCREAMING. HE REMEMBERS THE HOUSE ACROSS THE MAIN ROAD FROM US THAT WAS BLOWN UP BY A ROCKET. AND HE REMEMBERS HOW THE GRANDMOTHER OF THAT FAMILY SAT IN THE ROAD AND CRIED FOR TWO DAYS AND TWO NIGHTS. BUT THIS IS NOW GONE A LONG TIME. AND THINGS ARE BETTER AND SAFER NOW.

HERE IS A POEM THAT MY BROTHER WROTE. IN ENGLISH IT IS ODD, BUT I LIKE IT. HE SAID I COULD SEND IT TO YOU.

ON A KITE I HAVE PAINTED TWO
  EYES.

When the kite flies I see beyond the
   mountains.
And when I see the ocean I want to
   sit on the sand.
I want to hear the waves and watch
   the boats.
And now I pull my kite back to earth.

I have to stop writing now. But I am
glad to think that someone so far away
will hold this very paper in her hand, and
our same sun will shine light on the words
as you read them.
   May this letter find you and your
family well and happy, God-be-willing.

Your friend in Afghanistan,
Amira Bayat

For more than a minute Abby sat there, holding the letter. It wasn't like she never got any
mail, because she did—things like birthday cards
from her grandparents or reminders from the den-
tist's office, and every month she got something
from the local 4H Club. But this letter? This was

from a girl who lived in a place where a rocket could blow up the house next door, a place where avalanches echoed in the night. This was completely new.

Abby could see how hard the girl had worked on this letter. It was like every letter of each word had been drawn by an artist instead of written by a kid. There were no cross-outs, no eraser marks, and no spelling goofs—at least, none she could spot. Amira had even spelled the word "capital" correctly.

And Abby was amazed that a girl of ten was able to express herself so well in a foreign language. She herself knew a few words in Spanish, like "*buenos días*" and "*mañana.*" And she also knew how to say "*bonjour*" and "*au revoir*" in French. But that was it. This girl must be a genius or something.

Best of all were the three drawings that her brother had made. They were just done with pencil on some kind of typing paper, but they were wonderful.

The first was a picture of the girl's family, with a name written above each person. The mother, Najia, had narrow, stooped shoulders, but she seemed strong and graceful, her hands folded lightly together in front of her, relaxed, with her mouth and chin hidden by the scarf that also covered her head. The father, Zakir, was tall and thin, with dark eyes, bushy eyebrows, and a toothy smile, his face mapped by friendly wrinkles. He wore a dark vest over a long-sleeved shirt, and some sort of flat-topped, brimless hat that came halfway over his forehead. The girl, Amira, wore a head scarf like her mother, but her face wasn't covered. It was a sweet face, bright and open, a warm smile on her lips. Except she looked like she might be a little bit cross-eyed. And, looking more closely, it seemed to Abby as if the girl also had a runny nose. The brother's name was Sadeed, and he stood with his arms folded and his chin high. There was a powerful set to his jaw, and his eyes looked straight ahead, fearless, almost defiant. He wore a vest and hat like his father, and was nearly as tall.

There was also a drawing labeled "outside the front door." In the foreground, two goats grazed on low grass beside a dirt road. A pair of women walked beyond the goats. One of them wore a long dark dress that went from the top of the head down to the ground, completely covering her face. The other one was dressed like Amira's mom, with a long dress, a heavy coat, and a head scarf that covered everything but her eyes. The woman with the head scarf carried some kind of woven basket held against her hip with one hand. Out ahead of the women, a young boy used a short pole to steer a donkey loaded with a pile of sticks. On either side of the road, a jumble of low, flat-roofed houses staggered off into the distance. It didn't look much like Central Street in Linsdale.

And last, there was a sketch of the mountains, jagged peaks covered with snow, rising up and up, towering into the sky, making the lanes and rooftops of the village below look like an ant farm.

Rereading the letter, then looking more carefully at each picture, Abby felt ashamed of the letter she had sent to Afghanistan. As near as she could recall, she had spent about ten minutes on it. The letter she'd gotten back was so much . . . more. This girl named Amira had obviously spent a lot of time writing it, not to mention the work her brother had done on the drawings.

But Abby's feeling of shame didn't last. It was replaced almost instantly by determination. Because she decided that her *next* letter was going to be as good as the one she had just gotten, maybe even better.

When Mr. Carson arrived home from work around four fifteen, he thought he would have to call Abby in from the woods. But walking through the kitchen, he discovered his daughter in the family room, hunched over the card table, with maps and papers and encyclopedias spread out, scribbling into a notebook.

"Hi, sweetheart—what're you working on?"

Abby didn't look up. "Pen pal letter. Can't talk now."

Her dad smiled and went back to the kitchen to start dinner.

CHAPTER 10

# CELEBRITY

All the kids in the morning class knew about Amira's second letter, the one that had just arrived from her pen pal in America. It was a few minutes before the start of the morning session on a Tuesday in April, and they crowded around her, then shushed one another as she slowly read part of the letter out loud, translating from English. When she stopped reading, they begged for more, and pushed to the front of the group to get a turn looking at the envelope.

But not Sadeed. He sat calmly at his place on the first bench, bent over his notebook, pencil in hand.

Najeeb punched him on the shoulder and said,

"Have you seen your sister's letter, Sadeed? The envelope? It's *huge!* And the stamps? Amazing—all kinds of pictures!"

Sadeed sniffed. "It's fine for small children and blockheads to get worked up about something like that. I have work to do. So stop bothering me."

Najeeb shrugged. "Suit yourself. But one of these days your brain is going to crawl right out through your nose so it can get some time off." And he left his friend to his studies.

Mahmood called the class to order, but before starting the lessons, he said, "Amira, will you come to the front and talk about the letter you sent to America? And also tell us about the one you have just received."

Amira pretended to be shy for a moment, but then she walked right to the front of the room. And, watching from the corner of his eye, Sadeed could tell she was pleased to be the center of attention.

"Well," she said, "my friend in America is named Abby, and she's two years older than I am. And she has an older brother, and a mother and a father, just like me. She lives on a farm in the middle of the United States, in a place called Illinois. And she sent me a letter first, and then I . . ."

Amira kept talking, and all the kids in the class listened and craned their necks as she held up some photographs for them to look at.

But not Sadeed. He stopped listening, didn't watch. But most of all he tried not to become angry or let his feelings show on his face.

Because it was very clear that Mahmood had chosen to send *his* letter to America, not Amira's. So Amira had done almost nothing to create the fantastic letter the American girl had gotten, and now *she* was the one up in front of the whole class, acting like *she* was a great writer.

Despite his best efforts, Sadeed couldn't help hearing Amira as she prattled on.

"Girls in America are sort of different, but also the same. But my friend Abby's school is very different from ours, much bigger, too. And they have one special teacher who does nothing but teach the boys and girls how to climb straight up a wall!"

Sadeed forced himself to stop listening again and began to recite multiplication facts inside his head. And about three minutes later he was very glad when the teacher finally made Amira shut up and sit down.

But all morning long, whenever the teacher

was busy with the older students, Amira and her friends whispered about the letter.

And all morning long Amira was famous, and she enjoyed every moment.

And Sadeed didn't.

# CHAPTER 11

# A REAL PERSON

W hen he and his sister got home after school at midday, Sadeed said, "I should take a look at that letter. You'll have to send one back to her now. And I'll have to help you with the English again."

Amira held the letter behind her back. "Don't pretend not to care, my fine Sadeedy-doo. I know you *want* to read it. You can't *wait* to see what the American girl wrote. I saw you at school, acting like it's nothing."

Sadeed scowled. "Just give it here, or I'll make you write back to her all by yourself."

"Very well," Amira said with a smile, "since you're so *desperate* to read it. Because she *loved* your pictures. And your poem."

She handed him the letter and skipped toward the door. "I'm going to go help Mother with her sewing. So you can be alone with your girl-friend."

"Don't be a cow," he growled. "And come back soon. You've got to have another letter ready to send by tomorrow."

"Oh, don't worry," she said, "because I know you're *dying* to hear what I'm going to tell my friend Abby this time—all about my *romantic* brother!" And she ducked out the door before he could answer.

Sadeed sat on the charpoy and turned the letter over in his hands. Najeeb had not lied about the envelope. It was big, as large as a whole sheet of notebook paper. The postage stamps had been arranged in the upper right-hand corner, nine of them. It was like a miniature picture tour of life in America. One stamp featured a smiling Mickey Mouse. Another showed a baseball player. There was a painting of a crouching mountain lion, another of a silhouette of a large deer with huge antlers, another of a beautiful insect that had four wings, a big head, and a long thin tail that made it look like a helicopter. There was a stamp with an image of a girl leaping above the five rings of the

Olympic Games, another of the Chrysler Building in New York City, and one that showed a close-up of a bright yellow sunflower with a dark brown center. And in the center of the group was a stamp showing an American flag in the night sky with the moon behind it. Each stamp was a small work of art, and placed together, the effect was dramatic.

Reaching into the envelope, Sadeed pulled out three pictures that had been printed in color. The one on top was a photograph of Panjshir Province, the kind that Sadeed had seen on a TV news report, a picture taken by a satellite in space. The girl had written along the top of the page, "I love your giant mountains!"

The second photograph showed the richest, greenest cornfield Sadeed had ever seen. A man stood at the edge of the field, and the stalks towered above his head, each plant heavy with tasseled ears of corn. Behind him the land seemed to stretch on forever, with row after of row of green and gold plants. And above the picture she had written, "This is my dad in front of our cornfield last August. Can you believe how flat it is here?? Very boring."

The third image was smaller than the others, a

rectangle in the middle of the page. It was a family portrait, with four people standing in front of a red brick fireplace. And Sadeed knew this photo was a direct response to the drawing he had sent of his own family.

The girl had also written a name above each person. Her father, Robert Carson, wore a white shirt open at the collar, a dark blue suit coat, and a pair of tan trousers. He had brown eyes behind gold-rimmed glasses, a high forehead, and dark brown hair. He looked happy to be with his family.

Her mother, Joan Carson, was almost as tall as her husband. Her hair was more blond than brown, her eyes were blue, and she looked right at the camera with a confident smile, her lips red with lipstick. She was wearing a pale green jacket over a white shirt, and her trousers matched the jacket. In real life, Sadeed had seen only one woman dressed in trousers before, an aid worker from the United Nations who had come to the village about a year ago.

The older brother, Tom Carson, came next, and he had a wide grin on his face, as if he had just told a joke. He looked more like his mom than his dad, with reddish blond hair, blue eyes, and a sprinkling of freckles across his nose and cheeks. He wore a white shirt and dark trousers, and his wide shoulders and large hands made him look like he had done his share of work around the farm.

Last, on the right side of the group, was the girl herself, Abby Carson. She wore a long-sleeved white shirt tucked into a pale blue skirt, with socks pulled up almost to her knees. She was a lot thinner than her brother, with a narrower face, slimmer shoulders. She seemed tall to Sadeed, almost as tall as he was himself. And unlike that picture from the first letter where she had been clinging to a wall, now her face was aimed right at the camera. Dark brown eyes, like her father's. Her hair was not as dark as her dad's, nor as light as her mom's. She was smiling, but she seemed more annoyed than happy, no teeth showing. She looked like she couldn't wait to go and do something else. She had her arms straight down at her sides, her hands almost clenched into fists.

The letter itself was very different from the first one. First there was the paper, which was a rich, creamy color, and it felt thick and heavy. The handwriting was much easier to read because the American girl had used a pen with dark blue ink. This time the words had been written with care.

And looking more closely, Sadeed was surprised. Right below the date and the greeting she
had written a word in Arabic script—not made
very skillfully, but it was readable:

سلام

The word was "*salaam*"—which means "hello"
in Dari.

*A nice thing to add,* Sadeed thought. *Maybe this
Abby girl isn't such a blockhead after all.*

The letter wasn't too long, written on the front
and back of one piece of paper. But compared to
the first one, it felt like it had been created by a
whole different person.

First of all, thank you for
your interesting letter. You
should be very proud to know a
whole other language so well.
I also loved the pictures you
sent—such good drawings. I can't
wait to show them to my class
at school.
    Nice poem, too. I don't write

poems myself, but I know one
that was in a picture book
my mom used to read to me at
bedtime when I was little.

The rain is falling all around,
    it falls on field and tree.
It rains on the umbrellas here,
And on the ships at sea.

It's good, don't you think?
It's by a man named Robert
Louis Stevenson. He also wrote
adventure books, but I haven't
read any of them yet. I'm okay
at reading, but I don't like
sitting around. Mostly I love
being outside. I have a new
fort I'm building in a fallen
tree in the woods behind my
house. I'll take a picture of
it with my phone and send it to
you with my next letter.
    It's pretty hard to imagine

what it's like to live where you
are, but the pictures helped. I've
also looked on the Internet at
a lot of photos of your country.
And now I pay attention to all
the news stories on TV about
Afghanistan. There's still shooting
and bombs and stuff. But I'm
glad it's been safe in your village
for a long time now. I hope it
stays that way. And not just where
you are, but everywhere. Here's
another one of your words I'm
trying to learn how to write:

I really love the shape
of this word in Dari. It looks
more interesting than it does in
English: peace.

You asked about the picture
of me climbing. That thing I'm

on is called a climbing wall, and it's for learning how to rock climb. It's inside my school, part of my gym class I have every morning. My gym teacher says I'm a good climber because I'm strong and I don't weigh too much. And I love climbing because it's so hard to do it perfectly. Except I wish I had mountains like yours around here so I could climb on real rocks. Have you ever tried mountain climbing? Or any of your friends? Like I said, here in Illinois, the land is very flat and boring.

I've got to do my other homework now. If I mess up at all for the whole rest of this year, then I won't be allowed to move ahead to seventh grade. I know—very bad of me. But I'm doing better. And I think it's great that you like schoolwork and that you're a good student. Keep it up!

Oh, I meant to ask, do you have any pets? I would love to have a cat of my own, but my dad doesn't like animals in the house. But we have about six cats that live in the barn. So that's okay. Also, what's your favorite color? Mine is green.

And what color is your hair? My hair was really long until I was nine, and sometimes I wore it in braids that my mom wrapped around my head, sort of like a crown. Is yours long or short? Do you ever wear it in braids? Do you wear your scarf all the time, even when you're at home?

I'll be waiting for your next letter.

Your friend,
Abby

Sadeed sat there looking at the picture of the girl and her family, feeling how strange it was to have this contact with someone so far away. It was like these people lived on the moon, or in a whole other universe.

He stared at Abby's face, trying to connect the words he had just read with this girl he saw looking straight at him. And at that very moment, gazing at her picture, Abby Carson became a real person to him—someone who was intelligent, someone who loved being outdoors, someone who noticed the beauty of nature and the shapes of words. And her favorite color was green.

And it struck Sadeed that right now he probably knew more about this Abby Carson in America than he had ever known about any other girl in his whole life, including his own sister.

He looked up from the photograph, startled. Amira was staring at him. She had crept back into the house and stood there, a few feet in front of him.

She gave him an impish smile, with one eyebrow raised.

"What are *you* looking at?" he snapped.

"You," she said. "You *like* her, don't you?"

"Don't be a donkey. I don't even know her."

Sadeed reached for his notebook and waved Amira toward the place beside him on the charpoy. "And don't just stand there—sit down and tell me what you want to say. And be quick about it."

This time it didn't take Amira very long to dictate her reply. And she didn't try to get funny and say something to Abby about Sadeed. She was too good at judging her brother's moods to put herself in that kind of danger. She talked, he scribbled, and it was all over in less than fifteen minutes.

Then Amira left to go back and help her mother, and Sadeed put his notebook away and hurried off to his father's shop.

When he got to school the next morning, Sadeed went over to speak with his teacher. The man was standing outside by the doorway as he always did before class, watching to be sure that the play didn't get too rough, and that the older children didn't bully the young ones.

"Good morning, sir."

Mahmood smiled and said, "Hello. Have you and your sister got the next letter ready?"

"Actually, no," Sadeed said. "It's not quite done yet. But I can finish it when we go home at noon. And if you like, I can take the letter with me when I go to my father's shop at the bazaar and give it to the bus driver. That will save you a walk to the marketplace. If that would be a help. Or I can bring the letter back here to the school, and you can take it to the bazaar."

Sadeed felt like he was talking too fast, pushing out too many words at once. And when Mahmood narrowed his eyes and frowned slightly, Sadeed almost stopped breathing. Because he wanted his offer to sound completely normal and natural. And he felt better when the teacher's smile returned.

Mahmood said, "No, you go ahead and deliver the letter. That will be just fine," and he dug into a pocket on his vest and pulled out a crumpled Afghani bill. "Here, give this to the driver, for his trouble."

Sadeed took the money and nodded, then hurried off to join his friends, who were kicking a soccer ball around the piles of snow that still dotted the school yard.

At about three thirty that afternoon, a bright blue bus rumbled and clanked and sputtered its way into the marketplace. True to his word, Sadeed was there at the bus stop, waiting for it. Every square centimeter of the bus had been decorated with hundreds of bright aluminum pie tins, so the bus looked more silver than blue. At least fifteen men, four goats, a crate of chickens, three spare tires, and countless bundles of belongings and luggage were piled on top, all crammed within a rectangle of low iron fencing that rimmed the roofline.

And when all the arriving passengers had filed out the front and back doors or climbed down from the roof, and when all the departing riders had paid their fares and crammed inside or been pulled up top by helping hands, Sadeed went up the steps into the bus, bowed respectfully to the driver, and handed him the letter and the Afghani bill. "This is from Mahmood, my teacher," he said.

The man smiled and nodded. "Ah, yes— Mahmood. Very good. I'll mail this tonight in the capital."

Then Sadeed pulled something from his vest and said, "And this is from me." He handed the man another Afghani bill and another letter. "Also to be mailed in Kabul. All right?"

The driver shrugged. "No problem."

Sadeed bowed again, said, "Thank you," and dashed out of the bus back into the marketplace.

There was a steady stream of customers at his father's shop, and all afternoon Sadeed measured grain and weighed flour.

But in his mind he kept hearing what the bus driver said as he had accepted that second letter: "No problem."

Sadeed wanted to believe those words were true.

And for the time being, they were. "No problem." Completely true.

But how about in a week? Or two weeks?

Then it could be a different story.

# CHAPTER 12

# POSTINGS

There were four items on the to-do list for the pen pal project, and number three was very specific:

3. Using copies of the letters you send, plus the letters you receive, you will make a bulletin board display in the classroom. You will update your display as often as there are new letters.

Mrs. Beckland had cleared some space on the corkboard at the back of her room after she had given Abby the address of the school in Afghanistan.

So the next day, Abby used a classroom computer to make a banner with letters two inches tall and stapled it to the bulletin board.

## My Pen Pal in Afghanistan

Then she had downloaded a map of central Asia from the Internet, printed it out, stapled it below the banner, drawn a heavy black line around Afghanistan, and just north of Kabul she jabbed in a red pushpin.

She also found an image of the Afghan flag online, and she printed it out extra large, using the big printer in the art room. She wanted the flag to fill up a lot of the empty space.

And before she put her very first letter into the envelope, she had gone to the school library and made a copy of it. And she stapled the letter up on the wall.

For the first week the whole setup looked pretty dismal—a big banner with one little handwritten note hanging there below a crummy map and a huge black and red and green flag. And hardly anyone noticed the project, and nobody cared. At all.

Then, during homeroom on the morning

after she got her first reply, Abby made a copy of Amira's letter and hung it on the bulletin board.

When the letter from Afghanistan was in place, she also began hanging up copies of the pictures that the girl's brother had made.

And that's when three or four kids came to see what she was doing, all of them girls.

Abby's friend Mariah said, "Your pen pal *made* these pictures? Herself?"

"No," said Abby as she stapled the third one in place. "Her brother's the artist."

Mariah leaned in closer, looking at the family portrait. "And that's the brother, the guy on the end?"

Abby nodded. "Right. Sadeed."

Mariah said, "Don't you think he's *cute*?"

Abby shrugged. "Yeah, I guess so."

McKenna gasped. "*Eew*—did you read this part in her letter where she tells about the rocket that blew up and *killed* people? Right across the street from her house?"

That information got a handful of boys up out of their chairs. And suddenly more than a dozen kids were checking out Abby's pen pal bulletin board.

"So, did you write her back yet?" Mariah asked.

"Because you're gonna put that up here too, right?"

"I wrote to her," Abby said. "But . . . I have to get it all ready. Before I put it up on the board . . . my second letter."

Which wasn't really true.

The night before, Abby had made copies of her second letter and the three pictures at home, and she had them in her book bag, plus a color copy of the envelope that showed what kinds of stamps she had picked out.

But with so many kids suddenly tuned in, she felt embarrassed. Because when she had been writing the letter to Amira, she'd gotten all caught up in it, and she had written things she probably wouldn't have—not if she'd remembered she was going to have to put it up on the wall at school for everyone to read.

She pulled Mariah over to her desk. "Here," she said. "Read this." And she handed Mariah her letter.

When she was finished reading it, Abby said, "I don't want to put that up back there. For everyone to read."

Mariah made a face. "Why not? It's fine."

"Don't you think it's too . . . personal? I mean,

that part about how I might get left back and everything?"

"Almost everybody knows that anyway," Mariah said.

Abby's jaw dropped. "They *do*?"

"Sure. It's not like you can keep your test grades a secret or something. And then you suddenly start doing every single bit of your homework, and then start in on some big extra-credit project? Dead giveaway. Besides, lots of kids blog and chat all the time, so your little bulletin board here is nothing. They blab about everything."

"Not me," Abby said again.

"Whatever," Mariah said. "Anyway, I don't think you should worry about putting your stuff up there. And you have to do it anyway. For your grade, right?"

"Yeah . . ."

"So just do it," Mariah said. "Get it over with."

And that's what Abby did. She walked right back there and posted copies of her envelope, and the letter, and the three pictures that went with it.

And Mariah was right.

Nobody made fun of her, nobody said much of anything about it. And a few minutes later,

Jill Ackerman even walked by her desk and said, "Great letter, Abby."

So Abby felt like the bulletin board part of the pen pal assignment was under control. She could deal with it. Whatever came in the mail, it would go up on the board. And she was going to write back to Amira and say whatever she wanted to, and just stick the letters up there for the whole world to see.

After all, she had nothing to hide. Nothing at all.

But just one week later, Abby was forced to rethink her whole privacy policy.

It wasn't because of the new letter she got from Amira. Because Amira's next letter was very ordinary, full of news about her school, and how she had shared Abby's last letter with all her friends, how she didn't have any pets, and how she couldn't wait for spring and summer to arrive. And about how she had never once wanted to climb a mountain in her whole life. No, Amira had not shared one thing that could be called sensitive or private.

But the same day *that* letter arrived, another letter came, also from Afghanistan. And the second letter changed everything.

CHAPTER 13

# SMALL MOUNTAIN

It was a Thursday afternoon, and Abby had just come home from school. And there on the kitchen counter were two letters from Afghanistan, both addressed to her. She recognized the handwriting on each envelope, and she was puzzled about getting two letters from Amira on the same day.

So she picked up one envelope, opened it, and read a simple, newsy letter from Amira. No photos, no poems, no drawings. The whole letter seemed sort of flat and lifeless—like soda without fizz.

As she picked up the second envelope, she yawned. It had been a long day at school, and as usual, she had a ton of homework. And now she also had two letters that needed to be answered. Then she thought, *Yeah, but at least this'll be a whole other letter I can put on my bulletin board. Which gets me that much closer to being done with this thing.*

So she tore open the second envelope, pulled out the paper, and began to read.

DEAR ABBY, AMIRA'S FRIEND IN AMERICA,

I AM SADEED, AMIRA'S BROTHER. AND I WRITE TO YOU BECAUSE I MUST TELL YOU THE TRUTH. THE TRUTH THAT AMIRA IS NOT REALLY WRITING LETTERS TO YOU, NOT ON HER OWN. I AM HELPING HER. SHE SPEAKS HER LETTER OUT LOUD TO ME, AND I COPY DOWN HER WORDS IN DARI. THEN I AM THE ONE WHO WRITES THE LETTER. IN ENGLISH. AND SHE SIGNS HER NAME ON THE PAPER WHEN I AM FINISHED. AND I HAVE TO TELL YOU ALSO THAT I HAVE ADDED WORDS OF MY OWN TO WHAT AMIRA HAS SPOKEN. SO IT IS LIKE WE ARE BOTH WRITING TO YOU.

AND THE LETTERS ARE EVEN MORE FROM ME THAN FROM MY SISTER. EXCEPT FOR THE LETTER YOU JUST GOT FROM HER. THAT ONE IS ALMOST EXACTLY AS SHE SAID IT OUT LOUD

TO ME. BECAUSE I KNEW THIS ONE TIME I
WOULD BE WRITING YOU THIS LETTER IN MY OWN
WORDS, SIGNED WITH MY OWN NAME. SO I
DID NOT NEED TO ADD ANYTHING TO AMIRA'S
LETTER THIS TIME.

HERE IN OUR VILLAGE, IT IS CONSERVATIVE.
THAT IS A WORD I KNOW. IT MEANS THAT
EVERYONE IS STAYING CLOSE TO THE TRADITIONS,
TO THE OLD WAYS, AND ESPECIALLY THE RULES
OF OUR RELIGION. AND HERE IT IS BELIEVED BY
MOST OF THE MEN WHO RUN THE VILLAGE THAT
A BOY OF MY AGE SHOULD NOT BE WRITING
LETTERS TO A GIRL OF YOUR AGE. SO WHEN
YOUR FIRST LETTER CAME TO OUR SCHOOL, MY
TEACHER GAVE AMIRA THE JOB OF WRITING BACK
TO YOU, BECAUSE THAT IS THE PROPER WAY.

BUT I WAS ALSO GIVEN A JOB. I WAS
TOLD TO BE SURE MY SISTER'S LETTERS MAKE
SENSE. BECAUSE IF SHE HAD BEEN WRITING
TO YOU ALL BY HERSELF, THE LETTERS WOULD
BE BAD. OR HARDER TO READ. AND YOU MIGHT
THINK THE CHILDREN HERE ARE BAD WRITERS.
WHICH IS NOT TRUE. AMIRA IS REALLY QUITE
BRIGHT. BUT ENGLISH IS HARD FOR HER, AND

**113**

for me also. But I have worked at it longer and much more than she has. I am the best student in our school at speaking and writing English. And I do not mean to boast, saying this. It is just to explain. And I think I have gotten better at English mostly by reading books.

Did you ever read a book called <u>Frog and Toad Are Friends</u>? It is a small book, one of the first American books my teacher ever let me read. It is simple. But very true in the way of friends putting up with each other. I have a friend, Najeeb, who needs a lot of putting up with. He is Toad, and I am more like Frog. I would read a million books in English. But my teacher has only a small boxful, and I have already read most of them.

I wanted you also to know I am enjoying your thoughts in your last letter. And I think it is a fine thing that you are learning to write words in Dari—Amira loves that too, but she forgot to tell you so in her new letter.

AND IT IS INTERESTING THAT YOU LIKE TO BE OUT OF DOORS. I ENJOY THAT ALSO, UNLESS IT IS TOO COLD. OR TOO HOT.

BUT I DO NOT SHARE YOUR LOVE OF CLIMBING ON ROCKS. MY UNCLE ONCE WORKED FOR SOME ENGLISHMEN WHO WENT TO CLIMB A TALL MOUNTAIN IN PAKISTAN. ONE OF THE MEN DIED IN A STORM. ANOTHER HAD BOTH HIS FEET CUT OFF AFTER THEY FROZE HARD AS IRON.

MY UNCLE SAYS THOSE CLIMBING MEN ARE CRAZY.

I DO NOT THINK THAT. BUT THEY MUST BE DIFFERENT FROM THE MEN I KNOW IN MY VILLAGE. BECAUSE A MAN WHO NEEDS TO MAKE A LIVING AND CARE FOR HIS FAMILY CANNOT THINK ABOUT CLIMBING A MOUNTAIN. IN MY VILLAGE, IT IS ENOUGH TO NOT BE KILLED BY THE ICE AND SNOW AND WIND OF THESE MOUNTAINS, AND TO GROW FOOD AND ANIMALS IN THE SHADOW OF THEM. THE MOUNTAINS LOOK BEAUTIFUL, BUT WE HAVE TO FIGHT WITH THEM, JUST TO LIVE HERE.

AND WHEN I SEE A GREEN FIELD LIKE THE ONE IN THE PICTURE YOU SENT, I DO NOT THINK IT IS FLAT AND BORING THERE. ONE

FIELD LIKE THAT WOULD POSSIBLY FEED ALL THE
PEOPLE AND ANIMALS IN MY VILLAGE FOR A
WHOLE WINTER. THAT FIELD IS BEAUTIFUL, LIKE A
SMILE OF GOD.

BUT SINCE YOU LIKE OUR MOUNTAINS, I
HAVE SENT YOU ONE. A SMALL PIECE OF ONE.
JUST A GRAIN OF STONE, REALLY. BUT IF YOU
PUT IT WITH THE POINTED END UP, AND GET
YOUR EYES DOWN VERY CLOSE TO IT, YOU
CAN SEE IT IS A TINY MOUNTAIN. I PICKED IT
UP TODAY FAR FROM THE ROAD. AND I THINK
NO OTHER PERSON IN ALL OF TIME HAS EVER
TOUCHED THAT STONE UNTIL I PICKED IT UP
AND PUT IT INTO THE ENVELOPE WITH YOUR
NAME ON IT. SO YOU WILL BE JUST THE
SECOND PERSON TO EVER HOLD IT.

ONE LAST THING. THIS IS A SECRET LETTER.
NO ONE MUST KNOW I HAVE SENT IT, AND
PLEASE, YOU MUST NOT WRITE A LETTER BACK
TO ME. BUT I WILL LISTEN TO HEAR IF YOU
SAY ANYTHING TO ME IN THE LETTERS YOU
SEND TO AMIRA.

AND I HOPE YOU DO NOT THINK I AM
BEING IMPROPER TO SPEAK TO YOU THIS WAY.

WITH RESPECT, AND WITH ALL HOPES FOR YOUR
GOOD HEALTH AND HAPPINESS,
  SADEED BAYAT


As Abby finished reading Sadeed's letter, her
heart was racing. And she wasn't sure why. Perhaps just because the letter was such a surprise.
But also because it was a secret.

She quickly read it again, and then looked in
the envelope for the piece of stone he mentioned.
Something had made little dents in the paper of
the envelope, but it was empty. And there was no
stone on the countertop, either.

She stood still a moment, mentally replaying
how she had torn open the envelope and pulled
out the paper. Then she got down on her hands
and knees, her eyes aimed straight down. And the
search began.

Muddy footprints. Crumbs from a muffin.
Dried drips of orange juice. A shriveled green pea.
A dusting of flour at the end of the counter where
her mom had rolled out some biscuits.

But no rocks or pebbles. Not even any grains
of sand.

Abby dashed to the mudroom, zipped open
her green backpack, and took out her flashlight.

Back in the kitchen, she turned off the overhead light so the floor was more shadowed, then stretched out flat on her stomach, pressing her left cheek against the vinyl tile. She lay the flashlight horizontal to the floor, and clicked it on. Keeping the bright beam flat and low, she scanned slowly from left to right. Five feet away, next to the leg of the breakfast table, she saw a tiny bump. She got to her knees and stumped over, keeping the light aimed at it. And she picked it up between her left thumb and pointer finger.

It was a piece of rock no bigger than half a kernel of corn.

Kneeling beside the table, she placed the stone near the edge and looked to see if it had a point. Yes. She turned it until the point faced upward. And bending over so her eyes were level with the tabletop, she squinted. And there it was, plain as day: a small mountain.

She picked up the tiny stone, got to her feet, and walked back to the counter. She put it into the envelope, then moved it around to see if it matched up with any of the dents in the paper.

Perfect fit, first try.

So now there was absolutely no doubt. Sadeed Bayat had picked up this very same little piece of rock. And he had sent it halfway around the Earth. To her.

And in the entire history of the world, exactly two people had touched this fragment of the Hindu Kush mountains: first Sadeed Bayat, and now Abby Carson.

Right then and there, Abby knew she was *not* going to hang this letter up on the bulletin board at school. No way. This one was personal. Plus, Sadeed had asked her to keep it a secret.

She opened the drawer next to the stove, pulled out a plastic zipper bag, and put in the envelope, the little rock, and the letter from Sadeed. For safekeeping.

And before she even got herself a snack, Abby ran upstairs to her bedroom, sat down at her desk, pushed aside the dictionary and the drill sheets from last night's vocabulary study, and grabbed a pen and a blank piece of paper.

She put the point of the pen on the paper, but then stopped. She leaned back and looked up at the corkboard on the wall above her desk. That was where she'd hung the four pencil drawings, the ones that had come in her first letter from Afghanistan. She looked at the family portrait, and at the boy standing on the far right side of the group, his arms folded, a confident look in his eye. And she couldn't help smiling a little.

Looking down, she wrote the date on the paper. Below the date she wrote, "Dear Amira," just like always. And thinking ahead, she knew she would be writing Amira's name on the envelope, too, just like before.

But in the letter itself, this time she would be speaking not only to the girl, but also to her brother, Sadeed.

And as she began the first sentence, Abby knew she was going to have to write two letters: one letter to send to Afghanistan, and another one that she could put up on the bulletin board at school. Without feeling embarrassed.

# CHAPTER 14

# CONNECTED

As the month of April ticked by, Sadeed wished more and more that he hadn't given his own letter to the bus driver that day. And if he could have taken it back, he would have. But the thing was done, and that was that. Now there was nothing to do but wait and see what would happen.

And why had he done this? Sadeed knew why, and he didn't like facing the truth about that. The main reason? Pride. And vanity. He wanted that American girl to know that *he* was the real letter writer, that they were mostly written by him, Sadeed Bayat. Because he didn't want Amira getting all the credit for his fine English and his excellent writing.

And another reason? Truthfully? Because it was a little dangerous. Because it was almost forbidden. And also because it was something new, something modern. Maybe the village elders would not give him a scholarship to go and study in Kabul, but he could still make his own connection beyond the village of Bahar-Lan.

*And really,* he reasoned to himself, *doesn't my teacher want me to be independent? And modern? Didn't he want me to be writing the letters to that girl in the first place? I know he did—I heard him say so right out loud!*

And Sadeed remembered also that it was Mahmood who had been giving him extra books to read, books that were not on the approved list from the Ministry of Education. And Sadeed had read them, understanding that his teacher was taking a risk to let him do so. Sadeed didn't even tell Najeeb about these books. Or anyone else.

These were books written in English, books from Britain and America. Sadeed had read *Robinson Crusoe,* and he had loved it—even though the shipwrecked sailor was a Christian and read from a Bible all the time. Still, he was a good man, and he was honorable.

And he had read *The Adventures of Robin Hood,*

and he had loved it—even though the good King Richard had been away in the Holy Land fighting the Saracens in the Crusades. But Robin Hood and his men? Noble. And Maid Marian? Beautiful and brave. And the Sheriff of Nottingham? A truly evil man.

The most modern book he had read in English was called *Hatchet*, an adventure story about a boy who had to survive on his own in a harsh wilderness. Sadeed had barely been able to breathe as he'd read that book, and he started wishing the story would never end when he was only halfway done.

And right now he was reading another novel, a difficult book called *Kim*, about a British boy in India who traveled about as a spy during the days when Britain had ruled that whole part of the world. Including Afghanistan.

All these books were so different from the books that were officially approved for English language instruction. *And who decided those books would be good for me?* Sadeed asked himself. *My teacher, that's who. So is it any wonder that I wanted to write my own letter to someone on the other side of the world? Of course not.*

And the letter he had sent to Abby the American? It was a bridge, a link. Not like using the Internet or a cell phone, of course. But still, it was real, a solid connection.

So on the Tuesday morning when the teacher handed Amira the new letter that had just arrived from America, this time Sadeed didn't try to pretend he wasn't interested. As his sister opened it, he raised his hand, and when Mahmood nodded, he stood up and said, "I would be happy to read my sister's letter out loud so that all the class could hear it."

Mahmood smiled and said, "And please, translate the letter from English into Dari as you read, so everyone can understand."

Amira slapped the letter into his hand and gave him a sour look.

Sadeed walked to the front of the room and tried to look confident. But translating from English this way? In front of everyone? But he began, speaking in Dari, slowly and carefully.

"Dear Amira,
    I hope things are good for you
there in Bahar-Lan. Thank you for
your last letter. It made me happy,
to hear about how you shared what
I wrote with your friends at school.

I have been doing that too. In my classroom, I put a copy of all my letters to you up on the wall. And then I also put up the letters you send back. It's part of the project I am doing. And the other kids here have started to pay attention now—thanks mostly to your good letters back to me. And the great drawings you sent.

I'm sorry that I keep talking and talking about your mountains, talking about how they are so wonderful, and how they would be so much fun to climb. Because I've done some more reading about mountain climbers, like about this group of British climbers in the Himalayas, where one man died in a storm and another had to have both his legs cut off from frostbite. So I understand that mountains can also kill people. And mountain climbing isn't always fun. And it's never easy.

Still, I think I just love the idea of climbing itself, of going up higher and higher, and being able to see so far away. When I climb on the wall

here in my gym, two other people
hold the safety rope for me, in case
I fall. And they have really saved my
life when I have slipped, right here
in my school gym class. Anyway, I
don't want to talk on and on about
climbing.

But I also like all the different
kinds of rope and the other equipment
climbers use. And I love learning how
to tie knots. There's this great knot
called the Alpine Butterfly that makes
a loop in the middle of a rope. It's
simple, and it could save a climber's
life. Very cool. And there's one called
the Prusik knot, and you attach it
onto a another rope. And you can use
two Prusik knots with loops for going
up or down on a rope, sort of like an
inchworm. And then there are the
metal links called carabiners, and all
kinds of little clamps and wedges. So I
like that part of it too. Sorry. I'm still
talking about climbing. I'll stop now. I
promise.

Here where I live the soil is so

rich, and the crops here love to
grow—as long as there's enough rain.
On my family's land we grow mostly
corn. The planting ended just a few
days ago, because the last week of
April is the right time to get the seeds
into the ground.

Anyway, this boy I know is really
smart, and he had this idea that I
could send you something. So I'm
doing that.

And what I've sent is a spoonful
of Illinois soil in a little plastic bag."

Sadeed stopped reading and reached into the
envelope. He pulled out the plastic bag and held
it up a moment.

"And if you pour out the soil,
then press it flat, and get your eyes
down close to it, it will be like
looking at our fields right now,
when it's all just dark, flat dirt. Not
like one of your mountains, with its
point up in the sky.

I picked up this dirt way back in

the woods near my new tree fort. Because my friend had that idea too, that I could send you something that no other person had ever touched before.

I really like that idea, that of all the people who have ever lived on the Earth, I am the very first one to touch this spoonful of soil. And now you are the second one. And then maybe your family, or kids in your class.

It's the kind of thing that makes you think. And my friend is so clever to have thought of this. And I'm going to thank him the next time we talk. But we don't talk a lot. Because it's not like he's my boyfriend or anything. Because I don't have a boyfriend. Because I really don't think—"

"Sadeed," the teacher said abruptly, "we thank you very much for your excellent reading. But now we must get on with our lessons." And he came and took the letter and the envelope and the soil and tucked everything into his vest.

Sadeed quickly took his seat on the front bench, then bent down, picked up his notebook, and opened it, flipping from page to page, eyes on the paper, looking very busy.

Sadeed was glad Mahmood had stopped him. He felt sure his face looked as red as pomegranate juice.

Because from the first words of the letter, he had felt as if Abby was speaking almost completely to him, answering his letter, point by point. But not so anyone else would know. She was plenty smart, this girl.

And she didn't have a boyfriend.

At that thought, Sadeed felt his face blush an even deeper shade of red.

As the lessons began, Sadeed hoped that at the end of the school day, his teacher would give Amira her letter back.

Because he couldn't wait to read the rest of it.

And then write a reply.

For Amira.

# CHAPTER 15

# FLAG

A mira began walking home with friends after school let out at noon, so Sadeed ran ahead. In his vest pocket was Abby's new letter, which his teacher had given to him as he left the classroom—along with a frown. And Sadeed knew that one day soon, his teacher would want to have a talk with him about his letter writing. But today, right now, he had a new message in his pocket from his friend in America.

Instead of following the main road to his father's house near the other end of the village, as he passed the front wall of Akbar Khan's compound, Sadeed turned left and walked along next to the high mud brick wall. Once behind the compound, there was only a scattering of houses, and the rocky land rose to a low ridge and then dropped away. He walked until he reached a path he knew, a shortcut that ran downhill, across a brook, then up to the ridge again close to home.

A week of bright, sunny days had melted a lot of the snow, so the path was mostly clear. He began to trot because he wanted to get home and finish reading the letter—before Amira showed up and claimed it.

Sadeed was headed downhill on the rocky path at a good clip when, just before he reached the brook, a stocky man stepped from behind an outcrop, blocked his way, then caught him by the arm before he could change direction.

"Ho there, speedy one. Where are you going in such a hurry?"

He spoke in Pashto, a language used by a lot of Afghans. His voice was deep and thick, and he had a firm grip on Sadeed's arm. His turban drooped down to the middle of his forehead, and his neck scarf was pulled up to cover his chin and nose. Only the eyes showed, shining hard and dark, framed by the upper edges of the man's beard. He had a big leather rucksack slung over one shoulder, and immediately Sadeed realized it was large enough to be hiding a rifle.

Trying not to show his fear, Sadeed thought fast. And then he replied, also speaking Pashto, "I've just come from the house of Akbar Khan. He does business with my father, Zakir Bayat. And I'm late for work at my father's shop. He's expecting me."

All these things were true, and anyone from within a hundred kilometers would respect the name of Akbar Khan. But the man kept hold of his arm.

"Well then," he said with a laugh, "they will both be happy that I've caught you, because I was sure you were going to trip and fall into that brook. Might have broken your neck. Or worse. And I'm sure both those fine gentlemen would want you to show some gratitude to the man who just saved you. Perhaps give him some food. Even a little money." Using his free hand, he began to pat Sadeed's pockets. "What's this?"

And before Sadeed could pull back, the man plucked the letter out of his vest.

"Aha, a letter," he said, a smile in his voice. "Heavy. Must be important."

As he turned the envelope over, his eyes flashed and his fingers dug into Sadeed's arm like a steel trap.

He cursed, then made a sound, as if he were spitting. "*The flag of America?* You have business with the people who pollute our land and murder us? Do you *spy* for them? In Helmand a boy like you was hanged by the neck for having American money in his pocket. Did you know that? And my friends would do the same to you. We should go visit them, you and this *flag*."

"It's—it's not my letter," Sadeed stammered. "It's to a girl—look."

The man squinted at the envelope, and Sadeed realized instantly that he couldn't read English. So he quickly pointed at the address and said, "See, it's to a girl named Amira."

The man nodded as if he had read it. "And who is Amira?"

"Just a girl," Sadeed said. "And the letter came from some other girl no one knows . . . and . . . and that girl wrote to Amira first. At school."

The man made the spitting sound again. "Girls in this village go to school? Just like in *America*! Shameful!" And he let go of Sadeed's arm, quickly ripped the letter once, then twice again, and threw the pieces to the ground.

Sadeed took off like a rabbit. He dodged the man's grasp, leaped the brook, and was halfway up the little hill before the last bits of torn paper had fluttered to the ground.

"That's right—run, boy," the man called. "And tell this Amira and the other girls to stay at home where they should. And tell that foreign girl her letters are not welcome here."

Sadeed looked back over his shoulder. The man had vanished—but a moment later he saw his turban bobbing among the rocks as he picked his way along the path that followed the stream up into the mountains.

Getting a fix on the man's location, Sadeed did a quick mental calculation. He turned, took a deep breath, and dashed down the hill. He jumped the brook, stooped down, picked up every scrap of paper, and then grabbed the ripped plastic bag of soil. He glanced up—the man was still making his way uphill.

He wanted to yell something brave and defiant, but instantly thought better of it. Stuffing everything into a pocket, he jumped the brook for the third time and ran back up the slope. At the first fork in the path, he took a sharp right. And in three minutes he was back among the houses of the village, and in four minutes he was back on the main road.

Only then did his heartbeats begin to slow.

His mouth was dry, and his breath came in rough gasps, so much so that an old woman beside a doorway said, "Child, do you need water?"

Sadeed nodded and stood panting on her porch while she ducked inside and came back out with a large blue mug. He drained it, said, "Thank you, Mother," and then hurried along toward home.

It was a lot to think about—the way the man looked, the feel of that grip on his arm, the way he talked, and how he hated America. He wasn't from around here, Sadeed knew that much.

And Sadeed was furious with himself, to have hidden behind his sister's name on the letter that way. *I should have told that guy that she had the right to go to school like anyone else. I should have kicked and punched and fought like a leopard. I should have pushed that man backward into the brook, then jumped onto him and tied him up with his own turban. And then delivered him to Akbar Khan, marching him right up the middle of the main road.*

Still, it was good to have gotten away. And to have gotten Abby's letter back too. *So really, the victory belongs to me,* he thought. *That man walked away with nothing!*

He got home, let himself in, and poured himself a glass of water from the large plastic jug in the kitchen. Then another one. And as he wiped his mouth, Amira came bursting into the room.

"My letter," she demanded, holding out her hand. "Give it here."

Sadeed shook his head. "I have to go talk to Mahmood Jafari. Something happened, something bad. And you have to walk with me back to where Mother is. Right now."

Amira stamped her foot. "No! I *want* my letter, and I want it right now!"

Sadeed reached in his pocket and pulled out the crumpled mass of letter and envelope and plastic bag. "Fine, here it is. This is your letter. Happy now?"

Amira's mouth fell open. Then her eyes narrowed and she pressed her lips together. "Who did that?" she hissed.

"A bully, that's who," said Sadeed. "And that's all I'm saying about it. I have to go and talk to the teacher. So out the door with you. Now. And no more questions."

And as they walked the stretch of road to the house where their mother worked with her sewing group, Sadeed kept his arm across Amira's shoulders the whole way.

# CHAPTER 16

# DECISIONS

A bulky man, you say?"

Sadeed nodded at his teacher. "Yes, but not old. About your age, I think. And strong. I've never seen him before."

Mahmood stood just outside the doorway of the school as the older boys and girls arrived for the afternoon session.

"And wearing a turban? Was it . . . a color?"

Sadeed knew what Mahmood was asking. He wanted to know if the man had been wearing a black turban. Because that's what some of the Taliban fighters wore. He shook his head. "No. White, or pale gray. And he went up into the hills, the trail beside the brook. He got very angry when he saw the stamps on the letter, the flags. And he spat and cursed America. And he said none of the girls should be going to school."

"Keep your voice lower, please," said the teacher, nodding to greet the last students arriving for the afternoon class—two girls. "I have to stay here, so you must go and ask for Akbar Khan at his home. Speak only to him, Sadeed, and tell him I sent you. And tell him what you told me. All right?"

"Yes, sir," Sadeed said.

"And tell this to no one else. And then go directly home."

"But, sir," Sadeed said, "I'm expected at my father's shop. To work."

"Ah, of course. And that will be fine. But first, find Akbar Khan."

Sadeed nodded and turned to go.

"And Sadeed?"

He turned back to his teacher.

Mahmood smiled. "You did well."

He nodded. "Thank you, sir."

The teacher went inside, and Sadeed walked briskly through the school yard, his chin held high, off to speak with Akbar Khan.

• • •

Sadeed obeyed Mahmood's order, and after talking with the headman, he told no one else about the incident by the brook.

But someone else must have spread the word, because by nightfall in Bahar-Lan, it was the talk at every dinner table in the village.

And it was the topic of discussion at the home of Akbar Khan as well. There had been only one serving of tea, but the seven men seated around the low table had already gotten down to business.

"I don't like to say I told you so," said Hassan, stroking his chin. "But I did. This letter-writing business was a bad idea from the start."

Mahmood was in no mood to be polite. "That's not the point. A stranger has threatened one of our village boys, plus all the girls who attend school. And for all we know, he has a band of fighters camped nearby. The issue is simple— the safety of the schoolchildren."

"Which would *not* be an issue," Hassan snapped, "if there had been no letters to and from America!"

Akbar Khan raised a hand. "Gentlemen, please— courtesy. I already notified the district police by radiophone, and they will make a careful patrol of the area in the next week or so. I suspect this is all a gust of wind. And it will pass. But until then, we stay alert. And keep our weapons handy. And our children will walk the main road to and from school, morning and afternoon."

"May I speak?" said Hassan, addressing the headman.

"Of course."

Making eye contact with each man in the group except the teacher, Hassan said, "I think it would be wise if the letter writing stopped. Because it is such a public thing now. Everyone will know if it continues. Word will get around. And why dangle red meat in front of an angry bear?"

Mahmood felt the thinking of the group tilt into agreement with Hassan. And he knew it was pointless to object.

So he nodded and smiled the most sincere smile he could manage. "I agree with Hassan one hundred percent. A wise decision. Except I do think we must send one more letter to the American girl. To explain. Out of courtesy."

The teacher was done speaking, but he held his hand out, palm up, asking for consideration as he looked at each man seated around the table.

And Akbar Khan said, "One more letter, to

be handled discreetly. A reasonable request. And during the next weeks, everyone stays on high alert. Are we all agreed?"

Everyone nodded, and the headman smiled. "Good. And now, more tea."

Even though Mahmood hated giving in to Hassan and his old, narrow-minded habits, part of him was glad about this decision.

The truth was, with Sadeed's involvement in the letters, and now with the American girl beginning to talk more about her feelings, it was a good time to stop, a wise time to stop. And it was also not such a bad thing that the most recent letter had been torn to bits before a person like Hassan could get hold of it.

It would be disappointing for the children, to have the exchange cut short. But this was a matter of putting safety first. Besides, Mahmood knew how to take the long view. Before too many years went by, every child in this village would have a laptop computer, he was sure of it. And he would use his defeat at today's meeting to win a more important battle some other time. He could afford to be patient.

Because he intended to be a teacher in this village for the rest of his life. And as sure as the sunrise, change would come. It would.

It just wouldn't be coming during the next few weeks, that's all. And Mahmood knew he could live with that.

He just hoped the children could be patient too.

# CHAPTER 17

# NOT STUPID

Z akir had also heard about his son's run-in
with the man by the brook, and as they
walked home after work and evening
prayers on Tuesday, both his father and his uncle
praised Sadeed.

"But I don't want any talk of this to your mother
or Amira tonight. They will know soon enough,
and I don't want them to be frightened."

So Sadeed and his family ate a good dinner,
and afterward he motioned to Amira. "Come,
let's try to fix up that letter from your friend."

As they walked to the far end of the room,
Amira whispered, "I know all about what happened to you this afternoon."

"You do?" Sadeed said. "Father said not to tell

about it, because he didn't want you and Mother to be scared."

Amira looked at him and made a face. "Do you really think anything ever happens in this village that the women don't know about—and usually *before* most of the men? *Mother* said not to talk about it, because *she* didn't want Father to be upset."

Working by the light of a kerosene lantern, they put both pages of Abby's letter back together, piece by piece, laid out neatly on the floor. Then their uncle went out the door, and a gust of wind blew it apart.

The second time, the puzzle seemed a little easier, and they assembled the letter on a small prayer rug laid on the charpoy, up off the floor and away from sudden drafts. They didn't have a way to fasten the pieces together, so Sadeed quickly copied the letter into his school note-book, word for word.

He stopped writing and said, "There. That's the whole thing."

Amira said, "Good. Now read me the rest of it. In Dari." She glanced across the room at their mother, still busy in the kitchen, and whispered, "Start near the place where she said she does not have a boyfriend."

Sadeed nodded and scanned his notes to find the right place. And as he began to read, he whispered too, because "boyfriend" was a word certain to get a reaction from his mother.

"I really like that idea, that of all the people who have ever lived on the Earth, I am the very first one to touch this spoonful of soil. And now you are the second one. And then maybe your family, or kids in your class.

It's the kind of thing that makes you think. And my friend is so clever to have thought of this. And I'm going to thank him the next time we talk. But we don't talk a lot. Because it's not like he's my boyfriend or anything. Because I don't have a boyfriend. Because I really don't think much about that. A lot of my girlfriends do, getting all crazy and everything. I mean, a couple of my friends are boys. But not boyfriends.

I wonder about the books you like to read. Because even though I don't read a lot of books now, when I was about six years old there was one called <u>Frog and Toad Are Friends</u> that I really liked. I probably read that book fifty times. Do you have it there? It's a book that's funny and smart at the same time. And I'm sort of like Toad, a little grumpy sometimes. And sometimes I start big projects I never quite finish, like all the tree forts I've tried to build in my woods here. Anyway, if you get a chance to read that book, you should.

I hope the days there are getting warmer like they are here. Actually, Linsdale is about 600 kilometers farther north from the equator than Bahar-Lan—I checked on Google Earth, which is this cool computer program. So spring might arrive there a little sooner than it does here. Except since you're up near the mountains, it might still be colder there. Or about the same. I'll try to keep track of the high and low temperature here every day until your next letter arrives, and you do the same, and we can compare.

Well, I've got to start my other homework now. I have a big test tomorrow in math, which is not my best subject at school. Truth is, I don't have any best subjects. Unless you count gym class.

Anyway, I hope you are well and happy. And your family. And I'll look forward to hearing from you again.

Your friend,
Abby"

As Sadeed finished reading the letter out loud, he had the same feeling he'd gotten at school—that Abby had been talking only to him the whole time. It was such a new thing, to be sharing thoughts like this. With a girl.

And he imagined Abby as a young child, sitting in a fine house in America, spending time with Frog and Toad, reading the very same words he had read, looking at the very same pictures. And he wondered if she had ever read the book *Hatchet. She should,* he thought. She would like it, especially the parts about how the boy made his own little house in the wilderness. Almost like a tree fort.

"I want to write back to her now."

Amira's voice brought Sadeed back to the room.

"What? Oh—no, it's too late. And the letter doesn't have to be ready until Thursday. We can do it tomorrow, right after school."

"Then let's make the farm field, like she said. With the dirt she sent to me."

"All right," Sadeed said. "I'll put it on a piece of paper."

"And I want to be the second one to ever touch it," said Amira.

Sadeed shrugged. "Fine with me."

But the truth was, he had picked up some of the soil that had spilled into his pocket from the ripped plastic bag. So he had already touched it. Second.

He laid a piece of notebook paper near the edge of the prayer rug on the charpoy, and then poured out the dirt, a small dark mound. With one finger, Amira gently pushed it around on the paper.

She frowned. "That's stupid. Doesn't look like a field one bit."

"Wait," Sadeed said.

He picked up a piece of the ripped envelope, and, using one edge like a tiny bulldozer, he plowed the dirt into a perfect little square, like a plot of land on a hillside in the Panjshir Valley.

"Now," he said, "get your eyes down very close, and imagine all the other fields around it. But look only at this one."

And Amira knelt next to the charpoy, got her eyes level with the paper, and squinted. She stared for about five seconds.

"It's still stupid."

"Here," he said. "Let me try."

Sadeed got his face down close to the paper. He looked at the soil. He was close enough to smell it—a deep, rich scent, almost like fresh mushrooms. And he had no trouble seeing a flat, dark field in the heart of Illinois. And he could see the slender girl with the short brown hair bending down in the woods to pick up this very same bit of earth. And he saw her put it into a bag and carry it back to her house in her pocket. To send to Afghanistan. To him.

"Well?" Amira demanded. "What do you think?"

Sadeed shook his head. "You're right. It's stupid."

And he picked up the notebook paper, folded it, then folded it twice more into a tight, flat packet with the soil safely contained.

And as Amira got up and went to do her homework, he tucked the packet into his vest pocket. It was a tiny piece of America, a secret message, sent to him by a friend.

And it wasn't stupid. Not at all.

# CHAPTER 18

# FLAG

As Amira and Sadeed finished putting the ripped letter back together, it was about seven thirty on Tuesday night in Afghanistan.

It was also Tuesday in Illinois, but it was about ten o'clock in the morning, and Abby Carson was walking into her language arts classroom.

The bell was about to ring, and as she went toward her desk, she glanced back at her bulletin board. She stopped in her tracks, frowned, then walked right over to her teacher. "Somebody messed up my pen pal display," she said. "They stole the flag."

As the bell rang, Mrs. Beckland said, "We can't talk about it right now, Abby, but stay a minute after class, all right?"

Abby sat down and got out her homework. For the next forty-three minutes she and all the other kids stayed busy learning how to identify the main ideas in nonfiction writing samples, and then make inferences and draw conclusions. They would have to do that when they took the Illinois Standards Achievement Test in less than a month.

After the class ended and the room began to empty out, Abby went up to the front and waited while Mrs. Beckland finished writing something in her grade book.

When her teacher looked up, she smiled and said, "All right. Now we can talk. First, I'd like to ask you to keep what I tell you to yourself. You can certainly talk to your parents about it, but I'd rather not have other students know, all right?"

That seemed like an odd request, but Abby nodded and said, "Sure."

The teacher paused a moment, then said, "I'm the one who took the flag down, Abby. I took it down because the principal asked me to. Mrs. Carver got a letter from a parent of one of the sixth graders. And the parent said that the Afghan flag was making this student feel 'uncomfortable'— that's the word the parent used."

Abby made a face. "But how could . . ."

Mrs. Beckland held up her hand. "The letter to the principal said that this student was telling the parent about your project, and about the letters from Afghanistan and about the bulletin board. And the parent and the student looked up some information about Afghanistan on the Internet together. When they saw the Afghan flag, they wanted to understand the words that are written on the flag. They learned that the words are actually a prayer that's an important part of the Islamic religion. And this parent told the principal that since the child knows what the words say now, the words should not be on display in a public school classroom because that prayer promotes one particular religion. There's also a picture of a mosque on the flag. And all this makes the student 'uncomfortable.' And also the parent. So the principal asked me to take down the flag. And that's the whole story."

After a moment Abby asked, "Which student?"

"Only the principal knows. She decided it would be best that way."

Abby turned and looked at the bulletin board. The missing flag left a giant hole near the top of the display.

Abby wanted to say something like, "Didn't

you argue with the principal? Didn't you tell her that the flag is only part of a report?"

But saying that would probably just make her teacher feel bad.

And, to be honest, Abby knew that the only reason she had put the flag there in the first place was because it took up a lot of space.

That was then.

Now she sort of felt like she ought to stand up for Amira. And Sadeed.

Still, it was only a flag. And she didn't want Mrs. Beckland to get in trouble.

So Abby turned back and smiled. "Well," she said, "it's no big deal. I guess I should just put up something else."

Mrs. Beckland nodded. "Maybe a picture of a village. Or the Hindu Kush mountains. You can choose almost anything."

"Except the Afghan flag," Abby said.

"Right," said her teacher. "Except the flag."

# CHAPTER 19

# MOSTLY SADEED

About two weeks later, Amira's next letter was waiting for Abby when she got home from school.

Dear Abby,
 I am sad to tell you this.
I am not able to send more
letters to you now. My
teacher says so. And he asks
for you please to not write
back to me, and my parents
also ask this. It is because of
some people here who do not
like America.

But I like America, and so does my family. Many others too. And I like you also.

I am happy you wrote to me. And glad. I liked all the letters. And I am hoping to when we can send more.

Please be healthy, and give my good wishes to your family.

Your friend,
Amira

Abby read the letter once quickly, and then again. This one was definitely from Amira herself—it wasn't even Sadeed's handwriting.

She stood there at her kitchen counter, trying to understand: This girl's teacher wanted them to stop writing letters? And her parents? And who were these people who didn't like America?

She couldn't quite get her mind around it. There wasn't enough explanation.

But she didn't worry too much about it. Because she was sure there would be a second letter, like before. From Sadeed. Probably tomorrow, or the next day.

And he'd explain the whole thing. And even if his teacher said they had to stop the letters, they could probably figure out a way to keep sending them to each other. Of course, only if he wanted to. Either way was fine with her. Because, really, it was just a school project.

So Abby made a copy of the letter and the envelope, and she took them to school the next day and put them up on the bulletin board.

And she waited to see if anyone would notice.

Mrs. Beckland was the first.

"Abby, I'm so sorry about that letter from Amira, that she can't write to you anymore. But I think I understand. I've been hearing a lot on the news about anti-American feelings in that part of the world. So it's probably a question of safety for Amira and her family." She paused a moment and then said, "Sort of hard to imagine, isn't it?"

Mariah said something too.

"No more pen pal, huh? Good thing you got enough letters to get your grade. So that's cool."

No one else seemed to notice, just like no one else had noticed that the huge Afghan flag had been replaced by a picture of two old tribesmen sitting next to a road. And Abby wasn't offended or bothered about it, that no one else said anything. Because after a day or two, even a really interesting bulletin board turns into wallpaper, and almost nobody sees it anymore.

Five or six days later, Abby stopped thinking there would be another letter. And after two weeks, she had pretty much stopped thinking about it altogether. Because it made her a little sad.

And Abby didn't think about climbing on the wall that much anymore. She had done a few of the easy routes to the top during gym classes in April, but then the days had started to get so warm. And the higher you climbed in the big gym, the hotter it got. So she hadn't tried the ledge route again. Too much work, and it wasn't any fun to get all sweated out during first period.

Besides, she had plenty of other things to do. The end of the year was coming up fast now, and the constant pressure of getting a B or better on every single test and quiz was starting to get to her. She had never realized how much hard work it took to get good grades. She had always thought that somehow kids like Jill Ackerman and Kendra Billings and some of the other honor roll students got good grades automatically, just because they were smart. Not true.

All the schoolwork had even kept her from

making progress on her fort in the fallen oak. And it also kept her from thinking about life in the hills above Kabul.

Still, as it got to be the end of May and then June, every now and then as she sat doing homework at the desk in her room, she would look up from her papers and books at her own little bulletin board, and she would look at the pictures Sadeed had drawn. And she wondered how he was doing over there in Afghanistan. And of course, Amira too. And her mom and dad.

But mostly Sadeed.

# CHAPTER 20

# PRESENTATION

Abby, let's not forget that you still need to give an oral report for your extra-credit project, all right? How about Wednesday?"

When Mrs. Beckland said that to her on Monday morning, Abby nodded and said, "Sure."

But on the inside, she groaned.

Because an oral report was the last thing she wanted to deal with during her last four days at Baldridge Elementary School. All the tests and quizzes were over, and she had kept up her end of the bargain: a B or better on every one of them.

The sixth-grade class was doing community service projects around the school on Monday, and there was a bus trip to the Lincoln Museum in Springfield on Tuesday, and then the last day on Thursday was Field Day, almost like a carnival. It was supposed to be a fun week.

Plus, she really didn't want to dig into the whole Afghanistan thing again. She had kind of let it all go, stopped thinking about it. About the letters. About everything.

But the report couldn't be avoided. It was part of the deal, if she wanted to go on to seventh grade. And she did.

So about ten fifteen on Wednesday morning, she took her index cards and a few display items and went to the front of the room and stood next to Mrs. Beckland's desk.

And after the teacher got the room quiet, Abby started her report.

"Parts of Afghanistan are very modern. In a lot of towns they get satellite TV and Internet. But in most of the country, there's hardly even electricity or running water. So life for most kids there is a lot different than it is for kids here.

And Afghanistan is really ancient. The capital city of Kabul has been

there for more than three thousand
five hundred years—which is about
eleven times longer than Washington,
D.C., has been a city."

As Abby got through the first index card, she
could see that the kids were not into this at all,
not that she blamed them. She didn't want to be
stuck in a hot, stuffy classroom any more than
they did.

So Abby flipped ahead a couple of cards.

"Afghan culture is still really
connected to its past. For example,
the Afghan national sport is called
Buzkashi. And it's played by two
teams of men on horseback. And
there's a dead goat, and they cut its
head off, and then stuff sand down
into its guts to make it heavy.

One way to play the game starts
with the dead goat on the ground.
The players all try to grab the goat,
and then keep control of it and carry
it around a post at one end of this

**165**

huge field, and then get it all the way back and into their goal at the other end. And everyone is always fighting and trying to get the dead goat. And the game can go on for days, and they fight each other with whips and other weapons, and sometimes players get killed. And if you don't believe me, look on the Internet. It's pretty crazy."

That got the kids' attention, but Abby decided to cut to the end of her report anyway, the part about the letters. And after reading the first few sentences, she stopped looking at her notes.

"If you looked at my bulletin board, you saw the letters I sent and the ones I got back, so I'm not going to tell much about that. But I'm supposed to tell about what I learned. From the experience.

"And I have to be honest. I don't think I learned that much. I learned that the kids there are mostly like us, with the same kinds of feelings and everything. And that wasn't a surprise. Because everybody talks all the time about how people everywhere are pretty much the same. And I think that's true.

"And really, I decided to write to a school in Afghanistan for sort of a stupid reason—because there are big mountains there, and I'm kind of into rock climbing. So I thought it would be fun to write to kids there, and they could tell me what it was like to have these awesome mountains all around them.

"Turns out they don't think the mountains are that great. More like a problem. They have avalanches, they can cause floods, they catch all the rain way up high, which makes a lot of the land down below too dry for farming. And the mountains make it really hard to get around, to go places. And to have wires for electricity. All kinds of problems. Plus, the mountains are perfect hiding places for bandits and terrorists."

She held up a large copy of the drawing of the family.

"This is Amira, the girl who wrote the letters. And this is her mom, Najia, and her dad, Zakir. And this is her big brother, Sadeed, and he's the one who drew this picture."

At this point, Abby paused. Because this would be the perfect moment to reveal the whole story of Sadeed, the part no one knew. About how he wrote her a secret letter. About how he was the one who actually wrote most of the letters signed by Amira. About how he sent her a little mountain. And about how she sent him a spoonful of American soil. And how her last letter on the bulletin board was not the actual letter she sent, how she had left certain things out.

But she looked out at all the bored faces in front of her and said nothing. Because that part of the project? It was none of their business. And it wasn't part of the deal she had made with Mrs. Beckland, either. That part belonged only to her.

She said, "You might have seen that the last letter from Amira says that she had to stop writing to me, and I had to stop writing to her. Because there were people there who don't like America. She didn't exactly say so, but it was probably because it could be trouble for her or her family if certain people there knew she had an American friend. Because not everyone there in Afghanistan likes our country. So part of what I learned is that people are simple, but the stuff going on around them can get complicated. And even dangerous. And that's the end of my report."

She picked up the big copy of Sadeed's family portrait, stuck the index cards in her back pocket, and went to her desk.

Mrs. Beckland said, "That was very interesting, Abby. Does anyone have a question?"

No hands went up.

"Well then, let's use the next half hour or so to clean out lockers. Quietly. And then it will be lunchtime, and then there will be a thirty-three-minute after-lunch recess, and then all the fifth and sixth graders will go to the auditorium to see a movie. And tomorrow is Field Day. The weather's supposed to be hot, so dress comfortably, because after homeroom, we'll be outside almost the whole time until early dismissal at twenty-five after twelve. And if your locker is already clean, just stay at your desk and talk with your friends. Quietly."

Abby had emptied her locker on Tuesday, so she stayed at her seat. But after a minute or two, she got up and went to the back of the room.

Piece by piece, she took the pen pal information off the bulletin board and then sorted all the paper into the recycling bins.

The project was finished.

# CHAPTER 21

# FIELD DAY

It was Thursday, the last day of school, and Abby felt like she deserved every bit of the fun she was having. Field Day was like an extra-long gym class, plus free refreshments. The sky was blue, everybody was laughing and running around, and Abby knew for absolute sure that this was her very last day at Baldridge Elementary School. It was going to be an amazing summer, and in the fall, junior high.

She was mostly hanging out with Mariah, which would have been more fun if Mariah had been a little more athletic. Her idea of fun was to sit somewhere out of the sun and talk about how funny or stupid or crazy or cute or delicious everyone else looked or acted or sounded or smelled. And because it was the last day, Mariah had brought her cell phone, and probably sent and received forty text messages before lunchtime.

Since Abby wanted to actually participate in some of the activities, she would loop back to Mariah every half hour or so. But after the huge tug-of-war, they did connect for lunch, because eating was something they both enjoyed equally. And while they were in line for the barbecued hot dogs, Mrs. Beckland came straight toward Abby with a letter in her hand.

Abby's heart skipped a beat, then began to pound faster than it had during the three-legged race. Because she knew what Afghan stamps looked like, and the letter her teacher was holding out to her had come from Afghanistan, no doubt about it.

"Hi, Abby. I'm glad I found you. This arrived at the school for you today. It's from my friend in Kabul, the teacher who helped me set up your pen pal project. She probably wants to know how that worked out for you. And it would be nice if you sent her a thank-you note sometime this summer. Anyway, here it is. I know I've already told you this, but you did a great job on your project, on everything else as well. Be sure to stop back here and see me sometime next year, all right?"

Abby smiled. "I will, and thanks again for all your help."

She folded the envelope and put it in the back pocket of her shorts. She tried not to feel disappointed, but she was. Instead of a letter from a friend, it was from some lady she'd never met. And it meant she'd have to write a thank-you note.

As Mrs. Beckland walked away, Mariah said, "Aren't you gonna open it?"

Abby shook her head. "Later. When I get home."

"Abby," Mariah said, "it's a letter from the other side of the world—come on, open it up now. Open it up and read it to me."

Abby pulled it out of her pocket. She took Mariah's hand and put the letter onto her open palm. "Here, you read it."

"For real?"

Abby nodded, and Mariah put one long pink fingernail under the edge of the flap and sliced the envelope open. She pulled out a folded sheet of paper and squinted at the yellow sticky note on it. "This lady has terrible handwriting, and tiny. Is this even in *English*?"

"Here." And Abby took it from her and read out loud.

"Dear Abby,
A teacher from the village of Bahar-
Lan stopped in at my office at the
Ministry of Education, and he asked
me to send this to you. It's from one
of his students.

Yours truly,
Maleeha Tahar"

Abby unfolded the sheet of paper and began
to read, but not out loud. Because she knew the
handwriting. It was from Sadeed.

DEAR ABBY,

I AM SORRY I WAS NOT ABLE TO WRITE
SOONER, BUT WE HAD A BAD TIME IN MY VILLAGE.
A DAY BEFORE AMIRA WROTE TO YOU IN APRIL,
A MAN BECAME ANGRY WITH ME WHEN HE SAW
THE FLAG ON YOUR LAST LETTER. AND HE MADE
THREATS.

AND THAT IS WHY IT WAS DECIDED THE
LETTERS SHOULD END.

THE PROVINCIAL POLICE CAME, AND THERE
WAS FIGHTING IN THE MOUNTAINS AROUND US.

No one here has been hurt, thank God.
But still, we may not write letters.

My teacher was going to Kabul on
business, and I asked him to send my own
last letter to you. He was not surprised
when I asked. He guessed that I had
written to you before, because of when
you talked of Frog and Toad in your last
letter. It seemed too great a chance to
him, that we should both like that one book.

I have news you will like. My uncle
Asif had some strong mountain rope from
his time working in Pakistan. And he has
given it to me for my twelfth birthday.

And on a holiday afternoon he took me
to a rocky place near our house where
the land falls away. He showed me how to
make two loops at the end of the rope.
For my legs. And then another loop for
around my middle. And when I stepped into
it, it was like what you had on in the
first picture you sent. And then my uncle
took the rope around his back, and told me
to go over the edge. It was ten meters

HIGH, ALL ROCKS BELOW. BUT HE IS STRONG, AND I KNOW HE CARES FOR ME, SO I WENT, FLOATING ON AIR A MOMENT, THEN WALKING BACKWARD DOWN THE WALL OF ROCKS.

AND WHEN I GOT TO THE GROUND, HE CALLED, "NOW CLIMB UP. I WILL MAKE SURE YOU DO NOT FALL. JUST CLIMB."

AND I DID. ALL THE WAY TO THE TOP. I WAS VERY TIRED AND THIRSTY. AND I COULD NOT STOP TALKING ABOUT IT.

MY UNCLE IS SORRY NOW THAT HE GAVE ME THE ROPE. HE FEARS I WILL TRY TO CLIMB MUCH HIGHER. AND I MIGHT. WHEN I SEE MOUNTAINS NOW, THEY MEAN SOMETHING ELSE. BECAUSE OF THINGS YOU SAID. I THANK YOU FOR THAT. HERE IS HOW THE WORD FOR "MOUNTAIN" LOOKS IN DARI. IT SOUNDS LIKE <u>KOH</u>.

کوه

I THINK OF YOU NOW AND AGAIN, ALWAYS WITH RESPECT. BECAUSE I ADMIRE YOU. I HAVE READ EACH LETTER FROM YOU MANY TIMES. I KNOW I WILL KEEP THEM. I HAVE TO SHARE

THEM WITH AMIRA, BUT THEY ARE MORE MINE.
I ALSO KEEP THE FARMLAND YOU SENT. AND
THAT I DO NOT SHARE. BECAUSE IF ONE DAY
I COME TO VISIT AMERICA, I WILL RETURN IT.
AND IF I EVER OWN MY OWN PIECE OF LAND
HERE, I WILL ADD IT TO MY GARDEN.


WISHING YOU EVERY HAPPINESS IN YOUR LIFE, I
REMAIN YOUR FRIEND,
SADEED BAYAT


"Hamburger or hot dog, dear?"

Abby had been shuffling along in the line at the food table while she read the letter.

She blinked and looked up into the face of a parent volunteer, a lady wearing a huge orange T-shirt and a hairnet.

But she didn't want to eat. She wanted to think. And there was too much noise around her.

"Um . . . I'll be back . . . in a while."

"Hey, I'm starving!" Mariah said.

"That's okay, you go ahead and eat. I'll find you in a few minutes."

"But I want to hear what that kid wrote to you."

"We can sit together on the way home, okay?"

Abby said. "It's almost time for dismissal anyway. I'll meet you at the bus lines."

And Abby turned and walked away, headed for the school building.

When she got to the south doorway, another lady volunteer smiled and said, "Restrooms only. They're right inside the doors," as if the kids wouldn't already know that.

Abby walked to the girls' room. But then she kept walking. And after another twenty feet or so, she glanced over her shoulder to be sure the lady wasn't watching. All clear. She ducked to her left, pulled a door open, and slipped through.

She was in the gym.

The lights were off, and the large, empty space swallowed the sounds of laughing and shouting from outside. The air was still and hot.

Abby walked toward the far end of the gym, straight for the climbing wall. And while she was still thirty steps away, she could see that the leg harnesses had been unclipped from the belaying ropes, and the safety ropes had been tied to a hook about ten feet up off the floor. The thick blue impact mats had been dragged away, stacked over in a corner.

Abby tried the knob on the door of the equipment room. Locked. Putting her face to the glass, she could see the gear stacked neatly on the shelves—chalk bags, harnesses, helmets.

And she wished with all her heart that she had found out sooner that Sadeed had made his own first climb. On real rocks. Because then she would have been in here pestering the gym teacher every day, pushing herself to master that stupid ledge. And then she could have written back to him somehow. To share a victory with him.

She wanted to rush out onto the playing fields and find Mr. Insley and drag him inside so he could unlock the closet and help her gear up. And then spot her while she went right to the top, right over that outcropping. Because she felt sure she could do it. One shot, straight up, right now.

She walked to the base of the wall and stood below the ledge, looking up. She put her right hand on a rounded handhold, and her left found another one, and she pulled herself up. The toes inside her tennis shoes instantly found holds, as if they had little brains of their own. And fifteen seconds later she was up on the wall, her feet higher than the hook where the safety ropes were tied. Her hands were sweating, and the grips felt slick, but she didn't care. Chalk or no chalk, she was going for it.

But after another foot, she made herself stop. Because climbing unprotected like this went against all her training. It was a sure way to get hurt.

And she didn't want to spend the summer wearing a plaster cast. Or lying on a hospital bed. Or being dead.

So Abby edged her way down, about six times more carefully than she had gone up.

Panting, she sat on the floor with her back against the wall and took Sadeed's letter from her pocket. It was damp with sweat. And she unfolded the paper and read it again, smiling. Until she got to the end.

Because when he wrote, "Wishing you every happiness in your life," it felt so final. Like a last good-bye. It felt like from now on, she would be going along one road in life, and he would be taking a different one.

The principal's voice blasting through the outdoor PA speakers brought Abby to her feet. It was time to go get on the bus.

When she got to the front of the school, Mariah was waiting. And when they got to their seat, Abby handed her friend the letter.

Mariah made a face. "How come it feels all, like, *moist*?"

"Just some sweat," Abby said.

"*Eww*, gross!" But Mariah unfolded the letter anyway and began to read.

After a minute she said, "You had another letter from this guy? It wasn't on the bulletin board. How come you didn't tell me?"

Abby shrugged, and Mariah went back to reading.

Because Abby did not want to discuss this, not with Mariah, not with anyone.

So she turned away and tried to tune out the noise on the bus—all the yelling and talking and laughing. Because it didn't feel like the last day of school anymore. It felt like the last day of something else. She leaned her cheek against the bus window and stared out at the farmland.

The fields alongside the county road had been planted for six weeks now. And from high up in the yellow school bus, they spread out in front of Abby's eyes, stretching off into the distance. The corn was already eight inches tall, endless rows and rows of it, bright lines of green against the rich black earth.

And Abby tried to remember what Sadeed had said.

In his first letter he had talked about the corn-field, the one in the picture she'd sent to him. What had he called it? Then she remembered—"like a smile of God." That's what he'd said.

And for the first time in her life, Abby really looked at the land speeding past her eyes in the June sunshine. She saw it through Sadeed's eyes.

And it wasn't flat and boring. It was beautiful.

## DISCUSSION TOPICS

Author Andrew Clements chose the state of Illinois in the United States and Afghanistan as the settings in *Extra Credit*. Why do you think Clements selected these locations? What kinds of differences between the two countries—cultural and otherwise—can you identify after reading the book?

On the first page of *Extra Credit*, Afghani student Sadeed thinks that his teacher is going to "recommend him for a special honor," but when he finds out that his teacher wants him to help write letters to a girl in America, he is very disappointed. Nevertheless, how does this letter writing eventually turn into a "special honor" for Sadeed?

The character of Abby is introduced in the story when she is climbing a rock wall in her school's gym. Are you surprised to find out that Abby is struggling in school after reading about her abilities on the rock wall? Despite her grades, do you believe that Abby is actually very smart? Why or why not?

Think about Abby and Sadeed. Do they have similar personalities? Also, compare and contrast their everyday lives by talking about the following: their homes, their schools, their teachers, and their parents. How are they alike and how are they different?

As pen pals, Abby, Sadeed, and Sadeed's sister Amira communicate the old fashioned way—by sending letters to each other in the mail. Why is this their only method of staying in touch? What are some conveniences Abby and her friends have in the United States that Sadeed and Amira do not have in Afghanistan?

The rock wall at Abby's school in Illinois and the mountains of Afghanistan are symbols in *Extra Credit*—they stand for something else. What do they represent?

Abby learns from Amira and Sadeed's letters that not all of the girls in their Afghanistan village are allowed to go to school. Amira is glad that her father "permits" her to go to school. How did this make you feel when you read this?

The connection between brothers and sisters is explored in *Extra Credit*. How is Sadeed's relationship with Amira different from Abby's relationship with her brother Tom?

In the novel, Sadeed writes to Abby that he only has one book in his home, and that his teacher has taken a chance by allowing him to read books that are not approved by the Ministry of Education in Afghanistan. What did you think about this?

Discuss how a writer uses "foreshadowing" in a book. How does Clements use foreshadowing throughout *Extra Credit*? Identify parts of the story where foreshadowing is present.

While reading this book, we learn that Abby and Sadeed are taking risks by communicating with one another. Why do you think Sadeed decides to correspond with Abby when he knows that it is forbidden? Do you think Abby realizes that her letters to Sadeed would create controversy at home and in Afghanistan?

When Abby gives her oral report on her project at the end of the book, her classmates look bored and uninterested. Imagine you are a student in Abby's class. Would you feel the same way about her report? Why or why not?

Abby is reluctant to do her extra credit assignment at first. But how was the project actually a good thing for her in the end?

By the end of the story, Abby and Sadeed have a greater understanding of each other's lives and cultures. What else do you think Abby and Sadeed learned from exchanging letters?

## ACTIVITIES AND RESEARCH

How much did you know about the country of Afghanistan before reading *Extra Credit*? Find out more about this country. Research the history of Afghanistan, and think about present-day life in this country. What problems does the country face today?

Start your own "Project Pen Pal"! Find and communicate with your own pen pal. Conduct research on the Internet to find organizations that supply pen pal names and information. Then, after a few months of correspondence, create a bulletin board similar to Abby's.

Think about the significance of the small rock Sadeed sends to Abby from Afghanistan, and the dirt Abby sends from Illinois to Afghanistan. If your pen pal were in another country, what would you send to them to represent your home-town? What might they send you?

*Extra Credit* is a book that celebrates the power of friendship. Make a list of other books you've enjoyed that celebrate friendship.

What would it be like to be a character in *Extra Credit*? Imagine if you had the power to jump into this book. Would you be a friend of Abby, Sadeed, or someone else? Why?

Read Arnold Lobel's story *Frog and Toad Are Friends*. Why do you think Clements chose this book to highlight in *Extra Credit*? Do you identify more with Frog? Or Toad?

Continue the story in *Extra Credit* after the book ends. Write about what you think happens to Abby and Sadeed. Do Abby and Sadeed get back in touch again? Do they ever meet? What does the future hold for Abby and Sadeed?

# NOT APPROPRIATE

Clay Hensley frowned at the paper on the table. It wasn't a very good drawing. He'd made tons of better ones . . . like that picture he'd made of the old man sitting on the bridge? Now, *that* was good—even won a prize. This drawing? It was okay, just a simple portrait. It wasn't going to win any prizes—but then, it wasn't supposed to. It was supposed to do something else. Soon.

Out of the corner of his eye Clay saw Mr. Dash get up from his desk. The class period was almost over, so the art teacher was beginning his inspections, same as always.

Clay squinted and kept working on the portrait, shading a little here, erasing a little there, trying to get the expression on the face just right—actually, trying to get the whole head to look right. It wasn't easy.

Ears were hard to draw. The nose, too. And eyes? Forget about it. Not like drawing a tree. Or a piece of fruit.

Mr. Dash was at the back of the art room now, talking softly, moving from table to table.

"You see there, where the mountains meet the sky? Your lines need to be thinner and lighter there—it'll make everything seem farther away. Good detail work on that tree in the foreground."

Mr. Dash had to be talking to Marcia. Clay was sure. She was the only kid in sixth grade good enough at drawing to get advice like that. Except for him.

Clay kept working on his drawing, but his hand was so tense he was squeezing the pencil. He picked up his eraser and made a correction . . . then he had an idea. He took his big brother's cell phone from the pocket of his jeans, carefully, so no one would notice—Mitch would *not* be happy if some teacher took it away from him. One-handed, he clicked to the camera function and took a photo of his drawing, then another. He slipped the phone back into his pocket and picked up his pencil again.

Mr. Dash was working his way along the tables in Clay's row now.

"Good improvement there, James."

The teacher shuffled a few steps closer.

"Those shadows? Don't push on your pencil—makes 'em look muddy."

"But I want them really dark."

That was BriAnne talking, two tables away.

"Then just use a pencil with softer lead—4B, or even 6B."

Clay pretended to be busy with his work, but he knew Mr. Dash was right behind him now, looking over his shoulder. He heard the teacher suck in a quick breath, and then hold it.

Clay began counting. One thousand one, one thousand two . . . The art teacher let his breath out slowly.

Then he spoke, his voice low and strained.

"Clay . . ."

Clay kept working.

"Clay, stop it. Stop drawing."

He turned around and looked up at Mr. Dash. "Why?"

"You know why, Clay. That's . . . not appropriate. Your drawing's not appropriate."

Clay put a confused look on his face. "You said we could draw *anything* today. And I wanted to draw a *jackass*."

Several kids laughed. The whole class tuned in,

and the kids sitting close tried to get a look at his drawing.

Clay had a hard time not smiling. He was already imagining how fun it was going to be to tell his brother, Mitch, about this.

Mr. Dash raised his voice a little. "Please don't say 'jackass.'"

Clay rolled his eyes. "Fine. I wanted to draw a *donkey*. A stupid-looking donkey, that's all. And *I* think it's good. Don't you think this is a really dumb-looking donkey?"

More kids started laughing.

Mr. Dash swiveled his head and glared around the room. "Class," he growled, "be quiet."

The room went dead silent. The art teacher was over six feet tall, with broad shoulders, huge hands, and a bright red beard that covered most of his face. No student ever disobeyed an order from Mr. Dash.

With one exception. Because Clay kept talking.

"I mean, c'mon, Mr. Dash. If you'd said, 'Whatever you do, don't draw a donkey wearing glasses today,' then I wouldn't have. But you didn't say that. So I drew a donkey wearing glasses. Who has a mustache."

Then Clay held up his drawing so everyone else in the class could see he was telling the truth.

It was all true. He had made a picture of a donkey with a mustache who was wearing a sport coat and a striped necktie and dark-rimmed glasses—a donkey that looked remarkably stupid. And funny.

But not a single kid laughed.

Because that long-faced donkey looked like someone, a real person—a man every kid in the room was scared of. Except for one.

Clay had drawn a donkey that looked like Mr. Kelling, the principal of Truman Elementary School.

# ON PURPOSE

Clay knew what he was doing. He'd made the drawing on purpose, he'd let Mr. Dash see it on purpose, and then he'd held it up on purpose so everyone else in the classroom could see it too—and that last action was important.

Because now Mr. Dash couldn't just give him a scolding and move on—no way.

Every student in the class had *seen* the principal looking like a stupid jackass, and once those kids got out of the art room, they would tell all their friends about the hilarious drawing Clay Hensley had made. And sooner or later, the principal would hear about it—he would. And, when Mr. Kelling *did* hear about it, he would come stomping down the hall to the art room, his eyes blazing and his mustache twitching, and he would demand to know why Mr. Dash hadn't *done* something about that terrible boy and his terrible behavior.

So Mr. Dash had to do something. Clay was sure about that.

Would the art teacher keep him after school? Clay didn't care—as long as he got home in time for dinner. Mitch was going to be there tonight, and in a way, the more stuff that happened now, the better. He'd have that much more of a story to tell his big brother. Detention in the art room? No problem.

But Clay didn't think that was going to happen. It was Friday, a warm, sunny October day, and he had seen Mr. Dash ride his big motorcycle into the school parking lot this morning. It was perfect weather for cruising, and the back roads of Belden County were going to be beautiful this afternoon. The art teacher would *not* be staying late for a detention, not today.

Clay was pretty sure about that, too.

"Give me the drawing."

Clay handed it over, and Mr. Dash walked to his desk and took a large tan envelope out of a drawer. He slipped the drawing inside and sealed the envelope with tape. Then he picked up a marker and wrote on the front.

He handed the envelope to Clay and said, "Take this to the office and give it to the secretary. And then wait there until Mr. Kelling talks to you himself. Understand?"

Clay nodded, his face blank and serious. He didn't want to be disrespectful toward Mr. Dash. He was a pretty good guy. He was just doing what he had to, that's all.

As Clay picked up his backpack and headed for the door, every other kid was watching, studying his face, trying to imagine why he had made that drawing—and trying to imagine what Mr. Kelling was going to do when he saw it.

BriAnne whispered to James, and in the quiet room everyone heard her.

"Clay's really gonna get it this time."

# TO SEE AND BE SEEN

Getting from the art room to the office wasn't going to take long—maybe a minute. But Clay wasn't in a hurry.

He stopped at the water fountain and took a long drink.

He studied all the artwork in the display cases, including two of his own drawings.

He went into the boys' room and stood in front of the big mirror and combed his long black hair into three different styles. Then he combed it all back to his regular look—parted straight down the middle and tucked behind his ears, the same way Mitch wore his. Even though Mitch was seven years older, the two of them looked a lot alike, almost like twins—everybody said so.

As he came out of the washroom, a voice boomed, "Hey, get to the office *now*!"

Mr. Dash was standing outside the art room.

Clay waved and then ducked around the corner into the front hall. But he didn't go toward the office, not yet. He waited ten seconds, then peeked back around the corner.

Mr. Dash was gone, so Clay scooted across the open intersection and trotted halfway down the east hallway to the music room. He knew Hank Bowers had chorus now. He stood in the open doorway, pointing and nodding at other kids until they finally got his friend's attention. Then he made faces and scratched his armpits like a chimpanzee until Hank laughed out loud and got yelled at by Mrs. Norris.

Clay hooted, "Woo-wooh!" into the doorway, then ran back across the hallway intersection and arrived at the office just as the bell rang to end fourth period.

But he didn't go *into* the office. He kept away from the wide windows and leaned up against the tiled wall.

In his mind Clay began composing how he was going to tell Mitch about all of this later on. First was getting the idea for the drawing, then forcing Mr. Dash to send him to the principal with it, then goofing around in the empty halls and taking his own sweet time getting to the office. So far, it was a pretty good story.

A lot of the sixth graders were heading back from art and music now, and they were going to have to walk right past the office on their way to lunch. Clay had placed himself in the perfect spot to see everyone—and be seen.

He especially wanted the kids from his art class to see him standing there, to see that he hadn't even gone into the office yet, to see that the envelope with the drawing was still in his hand, still taped shut. They'd all be talking about his drawing, he knew they would. They'd be talking about what BriAnne had whispered to James: "Clay's really gonna get it this time."

And thinking about *that* brought the perfect smile to his face, the smile he wanted everyone to see, a smile that said, Yeah, that's right—I'm doing this *my* way, same as always.

While he was enjoying that thought and nodding at the kids who waved or caught his eye, Hank came up from his left and punched him on the arm.

"*That's* for gettin' me yelled at in chorus!"

Clay grinned and turned, then made a quick move like he was going to punch back. But he didn't. "It was worth it," he said.

Hank smiled, agreeing. "What're you waitin' here for?" he said. "Let's go eat."

Clay shook his head. "Can't. Gotta go see the warden."

"Yeah? What'd you do now?"

"I made a little drawing, that's all."

Clay opened the brown envelope—just ripped off the tape, pulled out the picture, and held it up.

Hank's eyes bugged out so far Clay thought they were going to pop and squirt slime everywhere.

"Oh, *man!*" he gasped. "You are so *dead!* Mr. K. seen that yet?"

Clay snorted. "What do *you* think?"

Hank stared at the drawing, then at Clay, and then suddenly seemed terrified, speechless.

"Yeah," said Clay with a grin, "after *that* jackass gets a good look at *this* jackass, I don't think I'll be hangin' out in the halls much, do you?"

Hank shook his head, and then kept on shaking it, both eyebrows up as far as they would go.

Clay started laughing, and when he noticed some other kids looking their way and pointing, he laughed even harder.

"Please hand that to me."

The deep voice was right behind him.

Clay stopped laughing. He turned around and gave the paper to Mr. Kelling. The principal looked at the drawing—and Hank slid three steps sideways and hurried toward the lunchroom.

The principal glanced up from the picture straight into Clay's eyes.

"My office. Now."

Clay nodded and walked toward the doorway, being sure to keep a cool, carefree look on his face.

But inside, he was actually grinning. This thing was shaping up just right—and he couldn't wait to tell Mitch all about it.

What's next from the
master of the school story?

# Turn the page for an excerpt from
# **Andrew Clements**'s new series!

Available now from
**Atheneum Books for Young Readers**

# PROMISE

As the ship's bell clanged for the third time, Ben ran his tongue back and forth across the porcelain caps that covered his front teeth, a nervous habit. And he was nervous because he was late. Again.

When she was being the art teacher, Ms. Wilton was full of smiles and fun and two dozen clever ways to be creative with egg cartons and yarn—but in homeroom she was different. More like a drill sergeant. Or a prison guard. Still, maybe if he got to his seat before she took attendance, he *might* not have to stay after school. Again.

The art room was in the original school building, and Ben was still hurrying through the Annex, the newer part of the school. But the long connecting hallway was empty, so he put on a burst of speed. He banged through the double doors at a dead run, slowed a little for the last corner, then sprinted for the art room.

Halfway there, he stopped in his tracks.

"Mr. Keane—are you okay?"

It was a stupid question. The janitor was dragging his left leg as he used the handle of a big dust mop like a crutch, trying to get himself through the doorway into his workroom. His face was pale, twisted with pain.

"Help me . . . sit down." His breathing was ragged, his voice raspy.

Ben gulped. "I should call 9-1-1."

"Already did, and I told 'em where to find me," the man growled. "Just get me . . . to that chair."

With one arm across Ben's shoulders, he groaned with each step, then eased himself into a chair by the workbench.

"Sh-should I get the school nurse?"

Mr. Keane's eyes flashed, and his shock of white hair was wilder and messier than usual. "That windbag? No—I broke my ankle or somethin' on the stairs, and it hurts like the devil. And it means I'm gonna be laid up the rest of the school year. And you can stop lookin' so scared. I'm not mad at *you*, I'm just . . . *mad*."

As he snarled that last word, Ben saw his yellowed teeth. And he remembered why all the kids at Oakes School tried to steer clear of old man Keane.

A distant siren began to wail, then a second one. Edgeport wasn't a big town, so the sound got louder by the second.

From under his bushy eyebrows, Mr. Keane looked up into Ben's face. "I know you, don't I?"

Ben nodded. "You helped me and my dad scrape the hull of our sailboat two summers ago. Over at Parson's Marina." He remembered that Mr. Keane had been sharp and impatient the entire week, no fun at all.

"Right—you're the Pratt kid."

"I'm Ben . . . Benjamin." He tapped his tongue against the back of his front teeth a few times.

The janitor kept looking into his face, and Ben felt like he was in a police lineup. Then the man suddenly nodded, as if he was agreeing with someone.

He straightened his injured leg, gasping in pain, pushed a hand into his front pocket, then pulled it back out.

"*Stick out your hand.*"

Startled, Ben said, "What?"

"You hard a' hearing? Stick out your hand!"

Ben did, and Mr. Keane grabbed hold and pressed something into his palm, quickly closing the boy's fingers around it. Then he clamped Ben's fist inside his leathery grip. Ben wanted to yank his hand loose and run, but he wasn't sure he could break free . . . and part of him didn't want to. Even though he was frightened, he was curious, too. So he just gulped and stood there, eyes wide, staring at the faded blue anchor tattooed on the man's wrist.

"This thing in your hand? I've been carryin' it around with me every day for *forty-three years*. Tom Benton was the janitor here before me, and the day he retired, he handed it to me. And before Tom Benton, it was in Jimmy Conklin's pocket for thirty-some years, and before *that*, the other janitors had it—every one of 'em, all the way back to the very first man hired by Captain Oakes himself when he founded the school. Look at it . . . but first promise that you'll keep all this secret." He squinted up into Ben's face, his blue eyes bright and feverish. "Do you swear?"

Ben's mouth was dry. He'd have said anything to get this scary old guy with bad breath to let go of him. He whispered, "I swear."

Mr. Keane released his hand, and Ben opened his fingers.

And then he stared. It was a large gold coin with rounded edges, smooth as a beach pebble.

Outside, the sirens were closing in fast.

"See the writing? Read it."

With shaky hands, Ben held the coin up to catch more light. The words stamped into the soft metal had been worn away to shadows, barely visible.

He read aloud, still whispering. "'If attacked, look nor'-nor'east from amidships on the upper deck.'" He turned the coin over. "'First and always, my school belongs to the children. DEFEND IT. Duncan Oakes, 1783.'"

Mr. Keane's eyes flashed. "You know about the town council, right? How they sold this school and all the land? And how they're tearin' the place down in June? If that's not an *attack*, then I don't know what is."

He stopped talking and sat still. He seemed to soften, and when he spoke, for a moment he sounded almost childlike. "I know I'm just the guy who cleans up and all, but I love it here, with the wind comin' in off the water, and bein' able to see halfway to England. And all the kids love it too—best piece of coast for thirty miles, north or south. And this place? This is a *school*, and Captain Oakes meant it to stay that way, come blood or blue thunder. And I am not giving it up without a fight. And I am not giving this coin to that new janitor—I told him too much already." His face darkened, and he spat the man's name into the air. "*Lyman*—you know who he is?"

Ben nodded. The assistant custodian was hard to miss, very tall and thin. He had been working at the school since right after winter vacation.

"Lyman's a *snake*. Him, the principal, the superintendent—don't trust any of 'em, you hear?"

*The principal?* Ben thought. *And the superintendent? What do they have to do with any of this?*

The sirens stopped, and Ben heard banging doors, then commotion and shouting in the hallway leading from the Annex.

The janitor's breathing was forced, and his face had gone chalky white. But he grabbed Ben's wrist with surprising strength and pushed out one more sentence. "Captain Oakes said this school *belongs* to the kids. So that coin is yours now, and the fight is yours too—*yours!*"

The hairs on Ben's neck stood up. *Fight? What fight? This is crazy.*

Two paramedics burst into the room, a woman

and a man, both wearing bright green gloves. A policeman and Mrs. Hendon, the school secretary, stood out in the hallway.

"Move!" the woman barked. "We're getting him out of here!"

Mr. Keane let go of Ben's wrist, and Ben jumped to one side, his heart pounding, the coin hidden in his hand.

The woman gave the janitor a quick exam, then nodded at her partner and said, "He's good to go—just watch the left leg."

And as they lifted the custodian onto the gurney and then strapped him down flat, the old man's eyes never left Ben's face.

As they wheeled him out, Mrs. Hendon came into the workroom and said, "I'm glad you were here to help him out, Ben. Are you all right?"

"Sure, I'm fine."

"Well, you'd better get along to class now."

Ben picked up his backpack and headed toward the art room. And just before he opened the door, both sirens began wailing again.